SPRING A

Spring was coming to the Lancashire countryside, but for Dr Tessa Daley the season had started cruelly with her tragic memories. Yet as she shared in her patients' joys and sorrows—and met a kindred spirit in Dr Adam Forrester—Tessa began to feel that perhaps there was still something in her that one day might blossom . . .

Lancashire born, Jenny Ashe read English at Birmingham, returning thence with a BA and RA—the latter being rheumatoid arthritis, which after barrels of various pills, and three operations, led to her becoming almost bionic, with two manmade joints. Married to a junior surgeon in Scotland, who was born in Malaysia, she returned to Liverpool with three Scottish children, when her husband went into general practice in 1966. She has written nonstop after that—articles, short stories and radio talks. Her novels just had to be set in a medical environment, which she considers compassionate, fascinating and completely rewarding.

SPRING AND DR DALEY

BY

JENNY ASHE

MILLS & BOON LIMITED
15–16 BROOK'S MEWS
LONDON W1A 1DR

First published in Great Britain 1986
by Mills & Boon Limited

© Jenny Ashe 1986

Australian copyright 1986
Philippine copyright 1986

ISBN 0 263 75344 1

Set in 10 on 11½ pt Linotron Times
03–0386–53,500

Photoset by Rowland Phototypesetting Limited
Bury St Edmunds, Suffolk
Made and printed in Great Britain by
Richard Clay (The Chaucer Press) Ltd
Bungay, Suffolk

CHAPTER ONE

It was a moist, misty morning. Tessa Daley looked out of her window in the doctors' quarters of Foxleigh Hospital. She had an uninterrupted view of a drab dewy field down to a patch of conifers wreathed in scraps of cloud. A large black and white bird rose suddenly with a clatter of wings. A magpie—one for sorrow. She watched it circle over the sad landscape for a moment, before it flew down into the trees.

The still grey morning suited her mood. After three weeks here, in the flat Lancashire countryside, her raw grief had lessened to numbness. Life held nothing for her now, without Guy. Her life stretched before her like the blank monotony she saw outside.

She dressed carelessly, jeans and a thick sweater. The room was heated, but the early March day was biting, and Tessa felt the cold. One of her delights, when she lived in London, had been wearing fashionable fun clothes off duty, but after Guy's death it didn't matter. Her one need had been to merge into the background, to hide herself where no one would see her sorrow, no one would get the chance to pity her. Foxleigh had been an ideal Registrar post—a remote Northern hospital, where she knew no one.

Guy's mother had been sweet; so had his sister Laura. They had been right to encourage her to get back to work. But they had been horrified when she chose to go so far away. 'Darling, what will you do for shops?' Gloria Trethowan had asked. And when Tessa had replied that she had lost all interest in shops, Gloria had hardly understood how anyone could manage without Fortnums on the end of a telephone.

Tessa filled the kettle. Even the drip from the tap reminded her of tears. She lifted it up with a strong movement and set it on the worktop to boil. She caught sight of her own wrist—slim and strong and shapely. Not like poor Sharon Billington in last Friday's clinic. A new housewife was Sharon, glowing with pride in her new husband, and fearful that the rheumatoid arthritis that had just been diagnosed would prevent her from caring for him, from living a normal family life—with children, and a dog, and Sharon doing the accounts for his growing haulage business in Preston.

And it was Tessa's job, as rheumatologist, to make sure Sharon's painful fingers didn't twist and bend helplessly, making her unable to care for herself. 'Will I be able to make a cup of tea, Doctor?' Sharon had asked. 'What about lifting, if we have a baby? I'm not very good at doing up safety-pins.' She wanted to manage her home, keep her husband at work, not by her side as she turned year by year into a helpless cripple.

Tessa put tea in the pot with healthy, swift movements. She ought to be thankful that she had no disability, no pain, as her patients had. But her inner pain was too shattering. At this moment she didn't care if she made tea or not, if she had pains in her joints or not. The clammy mists from the field seemed curled for ever round her heart.

It was Sunday, the day of rest. The intense silence emphasised her loneliness. She leaned back in the plastic kitchen chair and looked around at the bleak furnishings of the doctor's flat—functional furniture and the basic necessities. There was no personality here, no character.

She was an empty woman living in an empty flat.

There was the sudden noise of a door closing downstairs. She didn't know who lived down below her; it must be a junior. All the consultants were married, and living out Blackwood way, or even as far as Cheshire, so that they were near the golf clubs and the good schools. Tessa heard footsteps run lightly down to the bottom floor. She couldn't tell if it were a man or a woman. It didn't matter anyway; she couldn't bear to make empty conversation.

Then there came another sound, echoing nostalgically across the listening fields—the local church bells; real bells, not just one single note. Fancy having proper bellringers! Her sluggish imagination had been stirred, and Tessa stood up and automatically walked to the door and slammed it behind her. It was something to do. She would walk down to the village behind those conifers, and take a look at the church. A walk would pass the time as well as anything.

She didn't mean to go into the church, but the peal was still repeating its rather cracked notes as she reached the end of the hospital drive. It still clanged out as she reached the drab stone and brick village along the damp path still edged with last autumn's slippery leaves. She passed dour square houses, an ivy-wreathed post office, a garish modern chip shop, and a tiny white pub called the Brown Cow. The church looked old—dank and uninviting, with a squat tower, still ringing out its message. Tessa found herself walking in, her footsteps silent on yet more of last year's dead leaves, right up to the creaking arched door. Inside, the shadowy air of a million long-ago Sundays, dusty and hushed.

She slipped quickly into a pew at the back of the half empty church. The villagers sat as though ossified, the women in hats, the men's hair sleeked back with brilliantine, as they had been taught to do when they were boys, thirty, forty years ago, their collars dotted with dandruff. Tessa looked past them to the shiny silver cross on the altar. The last time she had been in a church was at Guy's funeral, surrounded by his family, and by his RAF colleagues. She felt again the numbness, the silent scream of disbelief and agony at his death. She would never get used to the waste, the terrible waste of his life, the golden life that had seemed so hopeful and so secure.

The vicar emerged, at the head of his assorted choir, then turned to his faithful flock: 'Dearly beloved brethren . . .' It was the old service—the prayer book that had been intoned here for centuries. Tessa found herself listening, as though hearing the old words for the first time. She might have entered a time capsule. The morning was suddenly ageless, dateless. 'Accompany me with a pure heart and humble voice . . .' What sin had she committed, that her beloved Guy should be snatched from her in a Harrier crash over the North Sea?

As she knelt on the squashy, worn cushion, she folded her hands together, but did not pray. Her eyes surveyed the reverent congregation, and saw in front of her a man who also knelt and did not pray. He too watched the congregation, with his head erect and unbowed. He wore a dark suit over a polo-necked sweater, and his hair was on the long side, and slightly dishevelled. His profile was craggily handsome, and his dark eyes smouldered under straight black brows. She sensed his disquiet; it equalled her own.

Tessa found herself wondering who he was, instead of listening to the sermon. Was he a regular? It was not likely that he, too, had slipped in on an impulse, as she had. The words of the Psalm nudged themselves into her mind: 'Have mercy upon me, for I am weak: O Lord heal me, for my bones are vexed. My soul also is sore troubled . . . how long wilt though punish me?' Suddenly Tessa thought of Sharon Billington, whose poor bones were indeed vexed. And for the first time since Guy's death, she found herself thinking of someone apart from herself. She bent her head and prayed—for Sharon, and for the torment of the man in the polo-necked sweater, who had stared at the stained glass window instead of praying.

She walked selfconsciously out of church. The vicar insisted on shaking her hand: 'Welcome to Foxleigh.' She was acutely aware of her jeans, her muddy shoes, her uncombed hair. She hurried down the path, not looking at the other people who assembled for a chat outside the door. But as she strode along the pavement, she felt a fraction—not happier, but lighter in her mind, for the act of having thought of someone else apart from herself. The damp of the early morning had also lightened. The paths were drying out, and there was a feeble gleam of sunlight through the grey, soulless clouds.

At least the morning had passed. As she retraced her steps, Tessa realised that the front door of the Brown Cow was wide open, and a light shone from inside, illuminating oak beams, little round tables, and burnished horse brasses. It was tempting. She went in, and found herself a corner seat, with half a pint of the local bitter. The landlord was a silent man, with a black beard. She was glad. She wanted no conversation, no signs of friendship—just anonymity, blending into her background. A sleek Irish setter nuzzled at her arm, and she patted the lovely creature and stroked its elegant head, sensing the smoothness under her fingers, and was rewarded by a liquid, soulful gaze.

There were four or five other people in the bar, all men. One sat alone, at the next table. Tessa was conscious that he was eyeing her when he spoke suddenly, in a broad Lancashire accent. 'You from round 'ere?'

She looked at him. Yes, he was speaking to her. He was small and nondescript, with pale eyes and eyelashes, and a shock of straw-coloured hair. He grinned, a grin without humour, and she realised that he was what might be termed the 'village idiot' in less enlightened times. She said, keeping her voice disinterested, 'I work at the hospital.'

He grinned again, and a sly look came into his watery eyes. 'You want to see the witches?'

She tried to ignore him, but he persisted. She said, 'What do you mean?'

He thought he had got her attention then, and edged a little nearer. 'The Foxleigh witches, down the road. Old Mother Crowe and her mates. Want to see?'

Tessa shook her head and turned away. Then she was conscious of a shadow across her table, and a tall figure was standing before her. 'Is he bothering you?'

It was a deep, reassuring voice, well bred and confident. She looked up into intense dark blue eyes in a swarthy, handsome face above a black polo-necked sweater—the man from church. He smiled slightly, acknowledging her look. She said, 'Not really.' She could look after herself, and the lad was not bothering her at all.

'She wants to come wi' me to t'cottage.'

'Scram, Billy.' The tall man spoke quietly, but Billy picked up his glass of beer and scampered to the other side of the room, where he sat crouched over the table, like a scared animal. The man turned to Tessa. 'He's simple-minded, but he can frighten people with his foolish talk. It seems to give him great pleasure to unnerve strangers with his stories of witches. He's convinced that the old lady in the white cottage is a witch, and someone told him the story of the Pendle witches, so he's connected the two ever since.'

Tessa nodded. The poor lad hadn't frightened her at all, and she wasn't in the mood for conversation. Apart from talking to patients, she hadn't held a long conversation with anyone, and didn't want to. She knew she ought to make an effort to pull herself together, but emotionally, she had put up a wall around herself, in an effort not to get hurt any more. 'He wasn't bothering me. Thanks anyway, but I guess I can look after myself.' She took a sip from her glass. The man didn't move away, and she looked up again into the dark face. He was regarding her very gravely. 'I said I'm okay,' she repeated.

He said quietly, 'You don't know me, do you? I'm just doing a neighbour a favour.'

'A neighbour?'

'I live in the flat below yours. Adam Forrester.' He held out his hand.

Not *the* Adam Forrester—the noted authority on small joint surgery? She hadn't even realised that he was based at Foxleigh. Tessa took his hand. 'I'm sorry, I haven't seen you around at all.' The handshake was brief and formal, but she found herself noticing the strength of the slim fingers, and the tanned skin in spite of an English winter.

'Well, you wouldn't, would you? You go around the hospital staring at nothing.' His voice changed from the gentle teasing note, when he saw that her expression remained stony. 'And I've been in the States for a couple of weeks.'

Tessa nodded. She didn't want to prolong this conversation. She respected his name—everyone in Orthopaedics and Rheumatology had heard of Adam Forrester—but she didn't need his company just now. And he sensed it. 'Excuse me.' He moved back to the bar and ordered a double whisky.

The setter nuzzled against Tessa's arm, and she patted its head again and picked up her glass. She didn't want Adam Forrester—or anyone else—breaching her private world of grief and loss. She bent her head, conscious that he was looking at her, and glad that she had not bothered to tie her hair back. It acted like a curtain against the interfering world in general, and Adam Forrester in particular.

There was a sudden surge of interest among the residents. Tessa smelt an expensive perfume wafting in from the dank grey morning, and looked up with scant interest, in time to see the entrance of an elegant woman in a well-cut dark green tweed suit. She had a sleek chestnut hairstyle, that reminded Tessa of the pedigree setter at her feet. She moved well, crossing the stone floor to the bar with assured strides. 'Morning, Adam.' It couldn't be his wife, if she said Good morning. An assignation, then. 'What are you drinking? Still Scotch? Do you never change?'

'No, Lorna. One of my few favourable attributes —I'm faithful.' Was that said with a rather cutting edge to the voice? Tessa looked away.

Lorna ordered a double gin. 'So, how's Foxleigh?'

'Still the same.'

'Glad to be back?'

'Slightly.'

'That's it, keep me guessing! How's the new rheumatologist? I hear she's rather a dish. Is she any good?'

The new rheumatologist. Well, yes, Tessa thought, she had been at Foxleigh only a week or so, but long enough for this woman to have heard of her. What would Adam Forrester say now? He looked across at Tessa. 'Come and meet her for yourself.' He crossed to Tessa, followed by the woman. 'Sorry to intrude again, Dr Daley, but I'd like to introduce you to Lorna Goodison, the local GP. You were bound to meet before long—Lorna takes a special interest in the problems of disabled housewives.'

Tessa stood up, conscious suddenly of her shabby appearance. The glamorous Lorna had been told Tessa was a dish. Well, she could see for herself now that Tessa posed no threat on the grounds of good grooming. Lorna must be her own age, twenty-eight, or perhaps a little older. The two women shook hands, murmuring politely. But they clearly had little in common, though Tessa hoped they would get on well. Lorna said, 'Sorry for barging in like that, Doctor. I didn't realise you two were together.' She didn't sound sorry; she sounded furious.

Tessa said quickly, 'We aren't together. We just met by chance. I was just out for a walk.'

Lorna Goodison said, her voice slightly warmer, 'There are some splendid walks around here. You're obviously the outdoor type. I'm sure you'll enjoy your stay here.' She returned to the bar, where Adam had already gone, and was draining his whisky glass, and the two of them continued to speak in low voices.

Tessa finished her own drink. She felt exposed. Far from blending into the background, she had now been well and truly introduced to all the onlookers in the bar, who had listened with unfeigned curiosity to all that had been said so far.

'Have another? On the house?' The landlord was standing by her, removing her glass. 'I didn't realise you were from the hospital. Nice to meet you, Doctor. My name's Browne, Sam Browne.'

'How do you do?' She accepted the half of bitter, but was glad the landlord was called back to the bar, and had no time to stop and chat. She didn't mind talking to patients, doing her clinics or ward rounds. But during the nightmare of the last eight months, she had avoided all other conversation. She had not wanted to interrupt her deep, wallowing suffering. She wasn't ready yet. Her grief had not yet run its course. Yet she knew that this morning she had been jolted just a fraction away from self-pity. She looked back at the craggy profile of Adam Forrester. He was magnetic, almost Heathcliffian in his majestic yet troubled presence. Strange that such a man was not married. Or perhaps he was. Perhaps the lovely Lorna was only a diversion.

Adam looked up at that moment and caught her gaze. For a second they looked at each other, and there was something—some form of kinship, or of understanding. Was it that they were both struggling with an inner problem? Or was it just that primitive look that a man and a woman exchange before deciding whether the other attracts them or not? Tessa was the first to look away. Leaving her glass half full, she slipped out of the door, almost eager for the raw chill of the damp air. At least it did not unsettle her, as human contact had done that morning.

She walked idly back, kicking at a small pebble, and trying to sort out the sudden turmoil in her mind. But the events of the morning were driven away by the appearance round a corner of a white cottage, and a small and very bent old lady, her parchment-like skin wrinkled into a million tiny creases, wearing a black beret on the straight, iron-grey locks. It took all Tessa's self-control not to leap back and gasp at the witch-like appearance. The crone grinned to her. 'Mornin'.'

'G-good morning.'

The old lady nodded blandly, and continued chatting to another elderly woman across the leafless hedge. 'No, our Jack can't get over today. Twins both got chicken-pox.'

'Aye, it's a long way from Liverpool wi' little ones. And she's expectin' another, you said?'

'There's one on the way. Not till the backend, though, and twins 'll happen be better behaved by then.'

It was the sort of conversation that could be heard in any garden in any village in the country. Not much black magic there, Tessa thought, as she strolled back along the soggy path towards the hospital entrance. She was glad she had made the attempt and come out for a walk. It had shaken her out of her deep hollow of depression, reminded her that there were other people in the world —some of them with problems. The memory of Adam Forrester's troubled face as he knelt in the shadowy church came back into her mind. What troubles could a highly successful surgeon have, coupled with his good looks, and an elegant lady friend? Her query was re-inforced as she heard the expensive roar of a powerful car behind her. She moved over into the moist grass at the side of the road, to allow the free passage of a shining white Porsche 928 which showed no sign of slowing down on the corner. It swooped past, and turned into the hospital drive. Tessa had a clear view of the occupants: the driver was Lorna Goodison, giving Adam Forrester a lift back. She pretended she hadn't noticed them.

*   *   *

This Sunday had helped Tessa a lot. Slowly but surely she came out of her shell, and got to know the hospital staff—at least by name, and at the level of smiling and asking how they were. Over the next two weeks she found herself coming back into the real world. It didn't change the deep, gaping wound of her bereavement, but it built up a protective cover for it. She went to the Brown Cow a couple more times. Sam Browne's quiet admiration was obvious, and they became unspoken allies in their mutual liking for quiteness and anonymity. The big landlord was taciturn and sympathetic. It was just what Tessa wanted at that time.

She also found that the immediate problems of mobilising arthritic sufferers became more interesting and rewarding, as she got to know her patients by name, and came to familiarity with their families and their particular problems. And her admiration grew for the relations, who stood by the afflicted one and rallied round, more often than not, to help and encourage.

She did not meet Adam Forrester much, and when they passed in the corridor, they exchanged only brief acknowledgements. Yet she found herself turning to watch his broad back in its white coat, the dark head she had first seen in the village church—and felt an affinity with. And then she would be ashamed of her interest, as though by looking at another man, she was betraying Guy's honour in some way.

On the third Sunday, Tessa found her way to the Brown Cow, which by now was becoming a dark and friendly place, suiting her mood. She could sit in the corner, almost hidden by a potted fern in a copper bucket, and feel protected and comfortable. It was midday, another dank and misty day. They had seen nothing but rain clouds and occasional flashes of pale sunshine. The trees remained obstinately bare, the buds unwilling to burst, though the official first day of spring was not far off.

'Join me in a whisky, Tessa?'

She looked up, startled. She had expected Sam Browne, but it was Adam Forrester, alone. 'Oh. Oh, hello.' She touched her half-pint glass, which still contained some local bitter. She only drank one, and made it last a long time.

'Mind if I sit here?'

She shook her head. She didn't mind, but she would have preferred him to sit somewhere else. She didn't come here to talk. All conversation was empty to her, unless it was to do with business. Adam sat down, and put two whiskies on the table, splashed with soda. 'You've referred a poor lass called Sharon Billington to me.' That was good; he was going to talk medicine. She didn't mind that.

'Yes. I know it's a bit early to think of surgery, but I thought in her case it might be wise. The disease is hitting her hard, and you know she's trying to help her husband in his business. The only alternative to surgery is bed-rest—and she can't spare the time, she tells me.'

'It's unfortunate,' said Adam, 'But I don't think we ought to replace joints at this stage.'

'Not right now,' Tessa agreed, 'I know it's too early. The ESR was over seventy last week. But I'd like you to see her regularly—and bring her in as soon as you think it's time. She's managing with the splints I prescribed for her at the moment, but if her fingers get too deformed —and it's happening all too quickly—then surgery will be that much more complicated, won't it?'

'You're right. I've injected the p.i.p joints anyway. That will keep her going for a while.'

Tessa nodded. It was good to have a colleague who thought as she did about cases. At the back of her mind, she was wondering why Adam was alone; usually he was with Lorna Goodison at this time. She went on talking, finding it easy, because it wasn't personal or disquieting. 'I've got the sweetest little lady in at the moment, bent completely double. Your Billy Blackshaw would say she was a witch. Pity she came so late, there's absolutely nothing we can do for her.'

'I know who you mean—old Lizzie Stott. She's a poppet. Sir Harold was going to do her hips—but her back is too far gone.'

'At least she isn't in any pain,' said Tessa. 'I've brought her in for a week or two for a rest, give her a taste of being waited on and pampered. Poor lady, she's waited on her husband and son all her life. Now she's widowed, and her son has found himself a wife, she deserves a rest.'

Adam smiled, and looked at her with his dark blue eyes, a direct look that disturbed her. 'You are good, you know. What made you come here from King's? You had a good chance there under Professor Mackeson. Surely you didn't give up the bright lights and a chance like that just because of Sir Harold Oliver's reputation? Good though he is, of course.'

He was getting near to the part of her that hurt—and without warning too. She felt her cheeks grow hot. She hadn't wanted this. She said hastily, 'It was either here, or join a commune on North Uist. I needed to get away.' She tried to keep her tone light. 'I decided to stick to rheumatology—I'm not sure how I'd cope at hand-weaving and porridge!'

The blue eyes searched her face keenly. Yet he did not go on with his questions—as though he understood without words how she felt. Through his shaggy quietness, Tessa saw something dimly that she liked quite a lot. He said, 'I think you made the right choice.' And she found herself blushing again, as though in some roundabout way, his words were a compliment. Then he said, 'Will you excuse me? I have a lunch date.' And she felt suddenly that she didn't want him to go.

Of course. She didn't need to ask who; Adam had heard before she did the roar of Lorna's Porsche. She watched his erect back, the country tweeds looking almost dapper on his military figure. He didn't turn back to her, and she found herself staring at the oblong of white sky in the open doorway he had just passed through.

'Another on the house?' Sam Browne was standing by her. She shook her head, and he picked up the two empty glasses and the beer tumbler as though to take them back to the bar. But he didn't go. He looked down at her with brown eyes as liquid and gentle as those of his pet setter. 'Now that's a man on the make, if ever I saw one,' he observed.

'What do you mean?' Tessa hoped she had not stared after Adam as though he mattered to her.

'That Forrester. He wouldn't look at that woman if she was poor. It's the Porsche he likes—and the fact that her daddy is a big noise on the local Health Authority. Oh yes, he knows where he's going, that one. He was furious when Sir Harold was promoted ahead of him.'

Tessa was surprised at the intensity of his tones. 'Hey, Sam, what's he done to you?'

'Well, for a start, he's leading you up the garden path.' The brown eyes were angry.

'No, he's not, Sam, honestly. We were only discussing a patient.'

'You can't tell me that. You said he lived in the next flat to you.'

Tessa nodded, uncomfortably aware that Sam Browne was jealous. 'Yes, but we hardly ever meet. It's not in my plan at Foxleigh, Sam. I want no personal relationships, with anyone at all.'

He said gruffly, 'Some hopes. Life doesn't work like that.'

'Maybe not.'

'I didn't want to get involved either. But I met a woman, and that was that. We had two good years, then we went to Rome for six months, and she went off with her singing teacher. I came back alone and without a job.' Sam spoke tersely. There was no hurt in his voice, only in his eyes.

'I'm sorry, Sam.' What else could she say?

'It doesn't matter now. But I ended up here, starting a new life.' He looked at her with sudden animation. 'Just like you, Tess.'

'I didn't say so.' She felt her heart miss a beat, at the second intrusion into her private life that morning. She was very thankful that Sam was called back to the bar. She had no intention of letting anyone get close enough for her to have to explain about Guy, and she detected in Sam rather more interest than she wanted. She stood up to go.

But just as she reached the doorway, Sam followed her, and she had to stop. 'Don't forget what I told you, lass. Forrester's on the make. He's after fame and fortune and a knighthood, nothing else. I see things from where I stand. I hear things. And I'm not daft at putting two and two together.'

'I'll remember.' She smiled casually. It was kind of Sam to warn her. But Adam Forrester meant nothing to her, so it didn't matter to her what his character was. All that mattered was that he did his job well, and was a good colleague.

Maybe it was the extra whisky, but as she came out into the cold March air, she felt invigorated and energetic. Instead of turning back towards the hospital, she made her way in the opposite direction, out into the country. There were scattered farmsteads and gently rolling fields. Tessa had thought Lancashire dull and grey, but as she turned up a farm path towards a ruined stone windmill on top of a small hill, she felt the tingle of the approach of spring. The branches were bare, but the catkins waved cheekily in the breeze, and under the trees were clumps of snowdrops. There was a vague tinge of fresh green, where the hawthorn hedges were just beginning to bud. She ignored the chill in the wind, and tramped upwards, feeling the beginning of relief and ease start in her heart. Maybe time was a healer after all. She laughed as she disturbed a pheasant, who waddled across the stony path just in front of her, a vivid patch of ginger feathers and a dark green tail.

She wondered, as she felt the elation of physical effort, what Guy would have thought of this cold, wild place. They had both been so happy in the bright dazzle of parties, theatres and clubs. The nearest to a country holiday was a day at the Cheltenham races. They had stopped at an inn, then wandered round the fields picking blackberries. And that night, when they got back, they had made love until early morning. Tessa shivered. Perhaps they had been too happy. They had exhausted their life's ration in the two short years they had been together . . .

The path opened out towards the top of the hill, giving way to rolling, rocky moorland. Patches of dead bracken dripped on the scrub and grass. The sky was cloudy, the clouds high and ragged, with streaks of pale blue temptingly revealed from time to time. Then Tessa saw the windmill, a stark stone ruin, with gaping holes in the sides, where the stones had been crumbled by the force of the winter gales.

She loved it—the wilderness, the signs of nature's cruelty side by side with the tender green in the hedges, and the upright pertness of the tossing snowdrops. She breathed in deeply, the fresh raw air, and turned round, to see the three-hundred-and-eighty-degree view of postage-stamp fields and dour farmsteads. The Irish Sea was out to her right, drifting into mist and grey haze at the horizon.

Then she gasped, and hastily took refuge behind a twisted oak, stunted by the winds. There, leaning against the windmill, stood Lorna Goodison. Her arms were wrapped tightly round Adam Forrester's neck, and she was pulling his face down to hers, so that his arms automatically enfolded her.

CHAPTER TWO

'HAPPEN you've taken my knickers from radiator, Barbara luv.'

'Nay, Lizzie, them's me own. I washed 'em last night.'

'So did I. You must've taken mine wi' yourn.'

'Nay, what would I want wi' your knickers, luv? I've plenty.'

'Let's see, then. Mine were Marks' best interlock —white. I got 'em special for coming in the 'ospital.'

'There, them's the same, happen. 'Ow many pairs did you bring?'

'Ee, lass, they're exactly same. Come on, Barbara, let's sort this out. Maybe you only washed one pair? Ee, you could 'a put your name on them! Then we could fettle this and no bother.'

'What about your name? It's shorter than mine.'

'Nay, it's not. Elizabeth is longer.'

'But Stott isn't. Stott's shorter than Shuttleworth.'

'Aye, that's true. Come over 'ere, luv, and we'll put 'em all out on the bed. 'Ow many vests did you bring?'

Tessa had walked into Ward H5. Sister Ainsley and the chief physio, Geraldine Wells, were standing in the office, almost doubled up with laughter. They didn't notice Tessa's entrance. Sister said, 'It's better than telly any time. Those two old ladies could bring the house down without even trying!'

The physio agreed. 'The Lizzie Stott double act, by special arrangement with Foxleigh Hospital Management Committee.' They looked on as the two old

Lancashire women carefully arranged their underwear along the bed. Lizzie was bent double—but her eyes were sharp through her iron grey fringe. She arranged the knickers lovingly with gnarled arthritic fingers, and Barbara Shuttleworth placed hers in an identical parade on the next bed.

Tessa said quietly, 'What's this? Kit inspection by Sister Ainsley?'

Sister swung round. 'Oh, I'm sorry, Doctor, I didn't see you come in.'

Tessa smiled. 'I know. You can't say you don't get entertainment in your job!'

'Did you hear the fuss?' The plump Sister's face was permanently cheerful, but this time her laughter broke out again. 'Aren't they sweet? I couldn't interrupt them for anything. That is—unless you're in a hurry, Dr Daley?'

Tessa shook her head. 'I wouldn't dream of interrupting either—I would hate to jeopardise the final legal possession of the knickers! But it might be an idea to put initials on them when they have sorted them out. If you leave it to them, they might both mark them "Mrs S."'

'I had thought of that.' Sister Ainsley began to be businesslike. 'Perhaps I'd better go and help. They aren't getting very far.' Indeed, both little ladies were now sitting side by side, identical pairs of underwear in their hands.

Tessa agreed. 'As I recall, Barbara Shuttleworth is in for bed-rest, but she isn't going to get any until she gets her own interlocks back.'

As Sister Ainsley went to the rescue, Geraldine smoothed down her neat tunic. 'I expect this sort of thing isn't quite what you're used to, Doctor? Your department in London was quite high-powered, wasn't it?' So the staff had been talking about her. Tessa didn't mind.

She nodded. 'High-powered, yes, but the results were no better. And somehow you seem to get a whole lot more fun out of it all. Is there something in the air here? Or is it just what I've been told is Lancashire folk?'

The physio seemed flattered. 'I thought you'd think us all rather slow, compared with your outfit.'

Tessa looked at her with a grave smile. 'This is my outfit—this, and Sir Harold Oliver. You can't deny he's the best in the country. Foxleigh hips are recognisable anywhere. And I know for a fact that one or two operations that went wrong in London clinics were sent here to be put to rights.'

'Yes, I know.'

Tessa looked back at the domestic scene before her, where Barbara was shuffling back to her own locker, her knees under the nightie swollen and disfigured. 'Yes, this is my outfit. I hope I can make something of it while Dr Bryn-Jones is away in Canada.'

'I hope you'll be staying on when he comes back?' Geraldine was not a demonstrative person, but it was a compliment she was paying, all the same. Tessa was gratified to see the pleased look on her face when she confirmed that she would like to stay on, if they would have her.

Sister came bustling back. 'Now, Doctor, what can I do for you? How about a cup of tea?'

'That would be nice. I just wanted to see Lizzie's notes, actually. Dr Singh was going to do a full physical for me. Has he done it?' Dr Singh was their houseman, a small, friendly Pakistani with a musical voice and ready smile. Sister brought out the notes, and Tessa sat down with a cup of tea at her elbow as she read up the all too familiar story of advancing disease, brought to medical notice too late to do anything to help the deformity and awkwardness. The sound of rattling teacups showed that the patients were being served their afternoon tea also.

Geraldine Wells had been watching through the window, idly sipping her tea. Suddenly she put her cup down so that it spilled. 'I say, Joyce, look at that. Just look!' She seized Sister Ainsley's arm. 'The tea trolley! It's exactly right.'

Sister looked at it with a quizzical lift of the eyebrows. 'Well, yes, Gerry,' she said drily, 'trolleys are designed to be just right, I'd imagine. Just right for putting cups and saucers on, and cloths for wiping up people's spills.'

'Oh, yes, sorry.' Geraldine mopped at the spill with a tissue. 'But just right for putting Lizzie Stott on too.'

Tessa looked up, interested. Lizzie had been a problem. They had tried Lizzie on a crutch, but her back was too bent. They had experimented with sticks, but her poor hands were not steady enough to control them. 'I think I see what you mean. A trolley on wheels, just high enough for her to lean on, would mean she could get about much better.'

Sister Ainsley smiled her agreement. 'And she could carry her knickers on the bottom shelf. It's worth a try, Gerry. Shall I ask Nurse Trent to go on safari in search of another trolley?'

'Yes, why not?' And it had worked—beautifully. Tessa left the ward with a warm feeling—not only of helping someone, but also the happy, relaxed human relationships she had been privileged to be part of. Foxleigh was turning out to be a much brighter prospect than she had ever dreamed possible when she first applied for this out-of-the-way place.

Next morning, she looked out at the bare trees against

the dull grey sky. It was the same scene she saw every
morning. Yet somehow, today there was something
different. For a while she did not realise what it was,
then she saw it—the definite tinge of delicate new green,
mantling the hedges, breaking the stark outline of the
branches. New buds were bursting, a real new year was
beginning.

Tessa felt a jerk of pain suddenly in her lower abdomen. Spring was coming. But what did it hold for her,
this timid, approaching baby year? Only memories . . .
She turned her thoughts briskly to the clinic she was to
take that morning. Only hard work would mask her
newly aroused feelings, that the season had cruelly
started in her, even though she was alone and without
love.

It was a routine clinic, mainly re-visits. There was one
new case, and Tessa's interest quickened as she saw the
signature of Lorna Goodison at the bottom of the blue
referral letter. 'Harry Ramsbotham—complaining of
severe pain in his back—usual analgesics have not
helped much—obliged if you would recommend a suit-
able anti-inflammatory therapy for him—kind regards
—' Tessa looked again at the letter. There was no
mention of an examination of the affected part, nor of an
X-ray.

Tessa sat up straight. This was by no means a good
letter; it was scribbled, as though in haste. It was not a
letter from a conscientious practitioner. But she must
not let her own personal feelings enter into this. Whatever the signature at the bottom of the page, this doctor
had not done her patient justice. 'Sister Coral, would
you arrange for Mr Ramsbotham to have X-rays of his
lumbar and dorsal spines? And hips too, while he's
there.' She signed the necessary forms.

'Yes, Doctor.' Sister bustled him off, with the traditional Lancashire mixture of bullying and kindness that came naturally to the women here, and made them such good nurses. They stood no nonsense, but their hearts were easily touched, and their affection readily expressed if necessary. Once again Tessa felt glad she had come here. It was so right for these patients—patients who would never get better, who knew very well they would never get better, who would need increasing care and help as they grew older. They wanted no pity, only practical help and understanding—and of that there was plenty around, something in the very air.

By the time Mr Ramsbotham came limping back with his X-rays, the clinic was empty, the rows of red vinyl chairs pushed askew by their recent crippled occupants. Tessa smiled a welcome as he came towards her. 'Now, let's see what we can do for you, Mr Ramsbotham.' She was surprised to see that his ruddy face was unlined. He walked like an old man, yet she saw from the letter that he was just coming up to fifty. He winced with pain as he sat down. Tessa took the X-rays from the nurse and studied them, pinning them up on the lighted frame.

'But there's no arthritis here!' The expression came out involuntarily, she was so surprised. Nurse Burrows moved over to look, and Tessa lowered her voice. 'The poor man had a fracture—look, that badly healed crack in L3. He ought not to be here at all.'

She turned round and sat at the desk. 'Now, tell me exactly when you first noticed this pain, Mr Ramsbotham?'

'It came on sudden-like. I was lifting bales of hay, last backend. When I got in, the wife thowt I was going to pass out, I went that white.'

Tessa made a quick note. The thought nagged her,

again and again, that Lorna Goodison had made a bad mistake here. If she had examined him properly, this fracture could never have been missed.

The man went on, 'So Dr Goodison gave me these 'ere codeine things, and she was very nice, considering the wife had to call her out just when she was going to a Council meeting. I went back when the pain didn't settle, and she tried me on some yellow tablets next —and then some that looked like rockets, and made me feel a bit—well, whoozy, like.'

'What did she say when she examined you the first time?'

'Well, she didn't rightly examine it, like, just asked me to point to where the pain was, and told me to come back if it didn't settle.'

There was a silence. Tessa pretended to be studying her notes, while she decided what to do. The poor man would have to be immobilised for a while. And the pain was much worse, because of the length of time that had elapsed since he first cracked that vertebra. There was even the possibility that he would develop osteo-arthritis here. She sighed. This was the kind of sad story she hated—a problem that could have been completely avoided by the correct treatment promptly given. She tried not to blame Lorna Goodison, but even if they had been bosom friends, she could not excuse the total mismanagement of this poor patient.

She examined his back, pressing as little as possible on the damaged spine. There was no doubt. If Lorna had examined him like this, the day she saw him for the first time, then it would have been clear that the trouble was traumatic, and not a rheumatic condition at all. Just because ninety-eight per cent of all cases of backache were nothing serious, it did not excuse the lack of proper examination at the first visit. Tessa's lips were set in a grim line of disapproval. She would have to let Lorna know; her opinion and advice had been requested. She took a deep breath and picked up her small cassette recorder.

'Dear Dr Goodison . . . thank you for referring Mr Ramsbotham . . . glad to confirm he has no rheumatic disease . . . ESR is normal, and RA latex test negative . . . X-ray shows a crack fracture at L3 with consequent strain on the adjoining ligament . . . therefore admitting him for rest . . . hope it will settle without the need for surgical intervention . . .' There. Had she been sufficiently cool and professional, and shown no sign in the letter of the fury that made her face white and her voice steely?

She watched as Harry Ramsbotham left the clinic, his face clouded at the thought of staying away from his farm, just when spring was here, the busiest time of the year.

'All right if I go to lunch, Doctor? I've put everything away.'

'What? Oh, yes, Nurse Burrows. Thanks very much.'

'You weren't too pleased with the last case, were you?'

Tessa smiled into the round face of the staff nurse. She realised she hadn't hidden her annoyance, but she mustn't let it become a talking point with the staff. She might not like Lorna—but no one must think that she was trying to score against her professional competence. 'Well, no one would like to walk around for six months with a broken back. But he'll be okay, he's a very robust chap.'

She walked along the corridor towards the dining-room. She had previously spent little time there, preferring to go back to her flat for a can of soup and a coffee in peace and quiet. Perhaps it was the approach of spring, and the residual anger about Harry Ramsbotham, that made her feel suddenly like a good meal, and a little company.

'Hello, Tessa. Long time no talk.' Adam Forrester was making for the dining room from the opposite direction. His white coat was flying open, and he was carrying a copy of the *Journal of Bone Surgery*. He stopped in front of her, and she could not help responding to his open greeting with a smile. 'Have you seen my article?' He indicated the journal.

'Well, I have skimmed through it. It's good—especially the latest advances in the materials used for artificial joints. Pity you can only get it in the States.'

'Well, I've spoken to a couple of British firms, but I can't say they're wildly enthusiastic, just cautious at the moment. But naturally, the Americans are so far advanced because of all they learned about polymers from their space programme.' He turned towards the tables. 'Will you join me, Tessa, or are you meeting someone?'

'Sure.' Tessa helped herself to a salad, and they sat together at a small table, the conversation never flagging. 'You go to the States a lot, don't you?'

'I must admit I think that's where I'll probably end up. I've had two firm offers of a Head of Department job, and one for a Professorship in Washington.'

'But you haven't taken anything up so far?'

'Not yet. It's only a question of time, I think.' And at that point, Tessa saw some of the anguish and bitterness she had seen in his face in church, when he thought no one was looking at him. There was something more than just professional advancement that was driving him to America.

She said quietly, 'It's easier to make that sort of decision when you're a bachelor. No one is depending on you, and you need no one else's opinion.'

'You're right.' But he made no further comment on that. Tessa wondered if Lorna Goodison knew that the handsome orthopod was not thinking of staying on. She studied him gravely as he cut a chicken sandwich into neat portions. For some reason—maybe the green fields outside the window, rolling past the pine forest into moorland—she saw him briefly as the tortured Heathcliff again, with his dark hair wild and his square face definitely poetic against the grey skies outside.

He looked up and caught her staring, and the tragic hero image vanished, as the dark blue eyes became suddenly amused. 'What's going on in your head, woman? You've been my neighbour for two months now, and I still don't really know what you look like. You're different every time.'

Tessa found herself responding to his gentle teasing with a smile. She looked down at once. Her defensive shield of grief had let her down! How could she let that happen so easily? She felt ashamed. How could she forget Guy like that, and respond to another man? She said quietly, 'You aren't supposed to know. I only exist as a doctor. If you can see my white coat, you can see all there is of me.'

'I don't believe you,' he said bluntly.

She felt threatened, unhappy. All she wanted was quiet friendship. She didn't want questions. Her voice was scarcely audible when she said, 'Please—?'

To her relief, Adam nodded. It was as though he understood. It was unusual to meet someone who seemed to be on her wavelength. Perhaps there was a chance of quiet friendship, after all. Before he went off to the States, of course. Tessa felt again the kinship she had first felt in church, seeing his dark head raised in anguish at something unknown, across the sleepy congregation.

She met his gaze then, and it was almost familiar. Here, she felt, was someone whom she could perhaps talk to—eventually. And then, suddenly, the ever-present 'Bleep, bleep' from the device in his top pocket. Tessa felt suddenly cheated, as he stood up. 'See you, then.' After he had gone, she sat staring at her coffee until it was completely cold.

Adam wasn't in the dining room at dinner time; she had seen him in the distance walking off with Mr Harrington, the consultant nephrologist. Perhaps it was just as well. Adam had been right—there was more to her than just her work, and tonight she was beginning to feel it. There was no disguising the fact that she had recovered from the first, ghastly shock of Guy's death. Sitting and brooding, giving in to her grief, had been the best thing she could have done. And now she was a person in her own right. All her hobbies had been Guy's hobbies—tennis, sailing, music—all they had done together. And now there was a void—a grey, misty void, that seemed as though it would never be filled again.

But at least she had come back to the real world. And spring was coming. Like the bare branches, that must feel the urgent approach of the new sap rising, Tessa felt that there must be something in her that one day might blossom. She had been through a winter the like of which she never wanted to experience again, but like the hedges that had looked dead, the appearance of death held only a promise of the return of spring.

She stayed chatting in the doctors' lounge after dinner. Usually she was glad to get away, glad to escape back to her own flat, her own misery, but tonight was different. There was a restlessness in her. Her own flat, a newspaper, the television—tonight it was not enough. Tonight she didn't want to shut herself away.

It was almost ten. She had stayed longer than ever before. She stood up and said good night to the few juniors who were still lounging around. 'Have some coffee?' someone said. But Tessa shook her head, and slipped out. She went up to her flat and threw open the window. It was chilly, almost frosty, with a few stars showing. Tessa impulsively pulled on her anorak and ran downstairs. A walk might get rid of her unsettled feeling, make it easier to sleep.

The night air was sweet-scented. The chill was there, but it was a fresh, positive coolness. The lawns around the hospital had been cut that day, and the smell of the mown grass was more beautiful than any artificial expensive scent. She breathed in great gulps of it, suddenly glad she was alive.

The lights in the Brown Cow were subdued but welcoming, like an old friend. Tessa walked lightly inside, rubbing at her nose, which was feeling the chill. 'Hello, Tessa. You're out late.'

'Evening, Sam. I just felt like a walk.'

'Must be spring. Clocks go forward on Sunday.'

'So they do.' The start of British Summer Time. Then there would be Mothering Sunday—and then Easter . . . the awakening of a whole new year without Guy.

'Half of bitter, Tessa?'

'Thanks.' She took her glass to her corner seat. There were only five others in the pub, two of them playing dominoes. She took a sip, and leaned back against the cushioned chair, quietly content to be only an onlooker of the leisurely activity.

It was then that she noticed Sam Browne's face. He was reading what looked like a letter. She had become used to this gentle giant, to his unspoken liking for her, his almost fatherly concern. She had not thought of his problems, so deep had she been in her own. But he was shielding his face from the public as he read, and she saw a tear trickle down the cheek, getting lost in the bushy black beard. Poor Sam! He had told her of losing his girl-friend to another man, but he had said it as though it was all in the past. This didn't look much like the past . . .

Compassionate, Tessa moved back to the bar and climbed up on to a stool. He had been there when she needed someone. Now she was in a position to help him, maybe. She waited until he had regained his composure, then she said cheerfully, 'Sam, you've been here longer than me. What do people do to pass the time of day around here?'

Sam managed a smile. 'Well, it's either Wigan Athletic or Blackpool. Some go for Manchester United.'

'Hmm. What do ladies do?'

'Wigan or Manchester United! Then again, there's an occasional point-to-point at the Manor. I suppose you haven't brought your horse?'

'No, Trigger's been pensioned off.' Tessa hadn't ridden since Pony Club days, and the attraction had worn off. 'Anything else?'

'Well—speaking for myself, there's music. There's actually more than brass bands in Lancashire, you know. We're not exactly savages.'

'I'm sure there is. Where do you go?'

'Sometimes Liverpool Phil. But it's quite a drive, and the chance of your battery being whipped while you're in there—or your tyres. I tend to go to the Free Trade Hall.

It takes half an hour—and I happen to like Manchester. But it isn't often I'm free in the evenings.'

'Your girl was a singer?' Tessa watched carefully. If he didn't want to talk, she could change the subject quickly.

But Sam didn't seem to mind. 'Yes, a good 'un. She taught music—that's where we met. I taught history at the same school.' He was silent for a moment. Tessa sipped at her beer, and didn't press the conversation. Then Sam came out of his reverie with a little shake of his head. 'Next time I'm going over, would you like to come to the Free Trade Hall?'

She smiled. 'Yes, Sam, I think maybe I would. And I've never seen Manchester. It would be nice to see a big city again afer all these weeks cooped up in Foxleigh.' Foxleigh could at times seem claustrophobic, especially, Tessa realised, when spring was coming.

'Then it's fixed. I'll be getting the programme at the weekend. Will you be in as usual on Sunday?'

'Sunday it is.' Tessa slipped from her stool. 'And you can remind me to put my clock forward.' She waved from the doorway, and set off back to the hospital, surprised at herself for feeling so very normal. It wasn't being unfaithful to Guy's memory, was it, to feel normal?

'Evenin', Dr Daley.'

Tessa started, then recognised simple Billy Blackshaw in the gloom. 'Hello, Billy. How are you?'

'I been to see Mother Crowe. The witches 'ave been at 'er, put the evil eye on 'er, like.' He lowered his voice to a whisper.

'Bully for you!' Tessa was used to him by now, and he could no longer frighten her with his wild, made-up tales of witches.

'You know who it was? It were Dr Goodison what

done it. She went to Briar Cottage, she did, and Mother Crowe, she hasn't walked to this very day. You didn't know Dr Goodison were a witch, now, did you?'

Tessa felt a strange hand grip her heart, but she kept her voice level. 'I'm sure she's not, Billy.'

'Aye, go on, don't believe me, then, don't. But it's true.' The idiot's voice rose to a whine. 'It's true, I tell yer. She's only pretendin' to be a doctor. You'll see.'

Tessa walked briskly past him. He was talking his usual drivel. Yet there was a vague sense at the back of her mind, that told her there might be a grain of truth in the lad's raving. After all, she herself had first-hand knowledge of Lorna's incompetence; there might well be more. Tessa could only hope that the GP didn't make a habit of prescribing painkillers without examination. It had happened once; it could well have happened on other occasions. She wondered what really was the matter with little Mother Crowe. She had seemed well when she saw her last at the cottage gate—thin and bony, but alert and well.

'And where have you been until this disgraceful hour?' Tessa looked up with astonishment as she mounted the last few steps to her flat. Adam Forrester stood leaning against the wall outside her front door. He smiled slightly, and came forward. 'No, love, I was only teasing. I'm glad to see you out and about, instead of hiding in your room. But I was let down. I just came back from an evening at Harringtons' and I was hoping you'd come down and have a drink with me. And there you were, gone.'

Tessa took out her key. 'Well, come in, and I'll make coffee.' The key came out, accompanied by tissues, paper clips, and a half eaten packet of mints. Adam helped her pick them up with a grin. 'It's really nice of you to come up.' She was flushed with the walk, and with the surprise of seeing him there.

'It's nice to see some colour in your face, woman.' Unexpectedly, he put out his hand and touched her cheek. 'I thought you were a little waif, when I first saw you, masquerading as a doctor.'

She was embarrassed, but pleased at the show of tenderness. She tried to hide it by joking. 'I'm really a witch, you know. My broomstick is in the meter cupboard. I've just got back from Mother Crowe's cottage.'

She was shocked at his expression. His handsome face darkened, the brows came together, and his hand dropped to his side. He stood for a second, then turned and ran noiselessly down the stairs.

CHAPTER THREE

IT was Saturday morning. Tessa woke slowly, aware that it could not be a working day, as she had not set her alarm. As she returned to full consciousness, she saw through her open curtains that the sky was a patchy blue, instead of the ever-present grey. She lazily swung her legs from under the duvet—and realised that the usual morning chill was absent. And her step was lighter than usual as she padded across the floor into the tiny kitchen, and filled her kettle.

Then she thought of Adam Forrester, possibly carrying out the same actions downstairs. She had been puzzled by his abrupt departure at the mention of Mother Crowe. For a while she had recalled the strange conversation with Billy Blackshaw, accusing Lorna of putting an evil eye on the old lady. Had Billy said the same thing to Adam, perhaps? That might explain his annoyance. He might have thought Tessa was making fun of Lorna—and he was fairly heavily involved with Lorna, there was no doubt of that. Tessa was glad, really. She liked Adam Forrester as a friend, but any suggestion of more than that would frighten her. She was glad she had seen them both, that windy day on the hill by the ruined windmill.

She took her cup of strong tea over to the window and gazed idly out. Yes, the morning was definitely Technicolor, not monochrome. The delicate blue of the sky made the dark green of the evergreens much prettier, especially as one or two pines were getting their light green new leaves. And to Tessa's delight, two—no, three—baby rabbits jumped out, and hopped rather unsteadily in a circle for a few minutes. Tessa set her cup down and watched them happily, until a squawk from a flock of rooks flying above them sent them scurrying for cover.

The telephone shrilled. So early? She was not on duty. She pulled her woollen housecoat more tightly around her and went over to answer it. 'Hello?'

'Tessa, my dear, is that you? How are you?'

'Oh, Gloria, how nice to hear your voice!' Tessa looked at her watch. It was nearly ten, so it wasn't really early for Guy's mother to be up and about. 'How have you been?'

'All right, dear. I suppose it will feel bad for a while yet. We've just come back from Madeira, and that took my mind off things for a while. But if it hadn't been for Laura, I'd have been pretty miserable, I suppose.' Yes, Guy's sister was sweet. And Tessa knew that having money didn't mean that Gloria's grief was any less than hers; all it meant was that she could go on holiday when she wanted, and try to fill her days with entertainment. Tessa felt that she was the luckier of the two, having a job that used all her physical and emotional qualities to the full, leaving little time for moping.

'So Madeira was nice?'

'Sunny, I must say. But, Tessa dear, how are you coping in that godforsaken place up among the slag-heaps? I can understand why you wanted to get away, dear—but you must wish you were nearer London.'

Tessa looked out again at the gentle sky, becoming luminous in the morning sun. And there—what was that bird? It was a lark, rising straight up from the dewy fields. She had never in her life seen a skylark before, or listened to its enchanting trilling song, full of bursting joy. 'I'm all right here, Gloria. I don't miss London yet. In fact, I'm getting quite fond of village life.'

'Well, don't stay there a moment longer than you want to, my dear. Laura just reminded me that Harrods are doing an Oriental Spectacular for spring—and Joseph's new lines are lovely this year. So do come down and spend a weekend with us soon. I really feel so awful, thinking of you all alone there. And Kleins were asking why they hadn't seen you this season. You remember that gorgeous grey flannel they made for you last year?'

'You're very sweet,' said Tessa. 'I will come and see you soon.' After all, they shared the same grief, and in spite of her society glitter, Gloria's heart was kindly in her own way. 'I think I'm going to Manchester next weekend, and then I have to be on call for the next two Saturdays. But I'll call you. Love to Laura.' She replaced the receiver with a slight twinge of remorse. How could she have woken and made tea and got so far into the day without even thinking once of Guy?

How could she be so unfaithful to his memory? They had been so good together. How could her first thoughts not be of him, after only eight months? It had been a glorious summer day when she heard the crackling news on her radio. A Harrier had crashed in the North Sea. Guy flew Harriers. But it couldn't be Guy; he was an expert pilot, just as he was a first-class prop forward and a Cambridge rowing Blue. He wouldn't have made a mistake.

A flock of birds, they had thought. The memories of the funeral were only misty pictures of grey and black, lots of people with sympathetic faces making sympathetic noises, patting her shoulder, telling her to be brave . . . And today, she had not even thought of him. Tessa went to the window again, the fields now dappled with the shadows of the trees, as the sun became bolder. A baby rabbit hopped out bashfully and sat for a moment, brushing at its nose with a small paw.

'Oh, Guy . . .' He was part of all this beauty now. She had to believe it. All his vigour, his love of life—it couldn't die. Perhaps she felt calmer because she knew he was now part of all that was lovely in nature? Somehow she knew he didn't mind that her first thoughts had not been of him that day.

Gloria's talk of clothes lingered at the back of her mind; Gloria was always immaculate. Tessa opened her wardrobe, and for the first time didn't reach for the nearest sweater, the usual jeans. She fingered through the clothes she had brought with her, remembering how she had loved wearing them, loved dressing up, making up, making herself desirable for Guy.

Tessa caught sight of herself in the full-length mirror. Not much glamour there, she thought wryly. The hair, once always glossy and neatly styled round her heart-shaped face, hung lifeless and neglected. Even the colour had changed, from a glowing nut-brown to a dull mouse. Yes, she had turned into a pale shadow of the girl she had been. Yet last night Adam Forrester had touched her hair with a gentle hand, and teased her into smiling into his dark blue eyes, and answering him back . . . What had he seen in her monochrome self to attract so much attention? After all, his Lorna was a vivid, compelling beauty. And she was rich. If Adam was really 'on the make' as Sam had said, then he didn't have to come up to ask Tessa to have a drink with him. What had he seen in her, that had brought them together last night in that brief moment of intimacy?

She showered, and washed her hair with a certain

amount of energy, toying with the idea of going into the nearest town to find a hairdresser. She wrapped herself in a bathrobe, and her hair in a towel turban. Suddenly there was a rap on the door.

Tessa pulled the bathrobe round her till it was decent, and opened the door a crack. Adam Forrester stood there, elegant in a three-piece suit and silk tie. She smiled, openly glad to see him. 'Good morning, Adam.' Her voice was as warm as the spring morning itself.

'I'm sorry to disturb you. I only came up to deliver this. It was put in my letterbox by mistake.' He handed over a buff envelope. Their eyes met as she took it, and the rather aloof look in his dark eyes softened as he looked at her.

'Thank you.' She pulled the robe tighter. He could easily have put it through the letterbox; it was nice of him to knock. 'I'd ask you in for coffee, but—'

'Thanks, but I'm working this morning.' Of course, the smart clothes, the tie. 'Five private cases at Larchwood.' That must be the private nursing home on the other side of Blackwood town.

'Of course, I should have realised—Thank you again.' Tessa closed the door and leaned against it, her heart thumping more noticeably than usual. Surely not at the sight of a good-looking man? No, of course not. It was the energetic shower and shampoo that had caused those palpitations . . .

She didn't exactly dress up after that, but she did wear a skirt instead of jeans. And she did take a little trouble with her hair, brushing it back from her face and securing it with a slide. She took a Jaeger jacket from its polythene cover instead of her usual anorak. Then she looked at herself. She had lost weight, and no wonder. But it didn't show too much, and she ran down the stairs, finding a genuine lightness in her step as she came out into the sunshine.

Her car was filthy. She hadn't used it once since she arrived, and it had been left out in all the dreadful weather. She tried the ignition with trepidation. It started at the third try. But how neglectful she had been! The battery must be getting flat. And it was scarcely possible to tell what colour the car was supposed to be under the layers of grime, splotched with rain and hail. Tessa drove through the village, and on along the country road towards Blackwood, the nearest town where she thought she would find a BL garage.

'Blimey, luv, where've you been with this?' The garage man was called George, and he was cheerfully direct.

'Oh, never mind the outside. I want it properly serviced, please. No hurry—I'll get the bus back. I'll ring to see when it will be ready.'

George grinned. 'It ain't that much bother to run it through the car wash, luv.'

Blackwood was small. Its streets had not been made for modern traffic. Tessa wandered along alleys with their original cobbles, to a high street that was the same in a thousand other country towns, with the usual cafés, record shops and chain stores. She was delighted to see a real open-air market in the main street—not Covent Garden, not Camden Lock, or the Portobello Road, but all the same, a real market, with the same mixture of tat and bargains that characterised markets all over the world.

At lunchtime, she chose the nearest pub to the market. It was called Potter's Bar, and it was fairly full of shoppers and farmers.

'Dr Daley? You all on your own?'

Tessa turned and looked up into the cheerful face of Sister Ainsley. 'Hello, Sister—I'm sorry, I don't know your first name. Will you join me?'

Thankfully, Sister Ainsley dumped a pile of shopping. 'It's Joyce. And thanks, I'd love to. Do you come here often?'

'Never been before. It just seemed handy. And my name's Tessa.'

'Well, you've made the right choice, Tessa. What are you ordering?'

'Just a cheese sandwich.'

'Is that all? Have some soup with it. Mrs Morris makes it herself, and it's wonderful. Believe me, I've been to France a couple of times, and her onion soup is the equal of any I've had. Morning, Mrs Morris.' The landlady obviously knew Joyce, and was introduced to Tessa.

'So you're a doctor? You don't look as though you've left school, lass.' Mrs Morris too emphasised the value of a 'good drop of soup', and Tessa was quite happy to take her advice.

Joyce Ainsley's husband worked in their market garden on a Saturday, she explained, so it was ideal for her to do the week's shopping, and treat herself to lunch out. 'I don't like to see you on your own. Don't you know any of the other doctors?'

Tessa smiled at her concern. Northerners were quick to feel compassion, and to express it. 'Oh, yes, I know them, but I had to bring my car to the garage.' She might tell Joyce about Guy one day, but not now. 'Do you know George's garage?'

'Oh, he'll do a good job for you. What car is it?'

'Metro—MG.'

'Nice. Not as posh as Dr Goodison's Porsche, eh? Have you seen that woman driving through the village at seventy? Stupid cow! If she loses her licence, there's be no one at all to do house calls. And some of them farms is quite a way out.'

'I thought she had another partner?' queried Tessa. 'I've had letters from a Dr Blake.'

'Oh, Tessa luv, Dr Blake's about ninety! He couldn't drive. So you see, she ought to use a bit of common sense, that one.' Joyce Ainsley's voice was tart. She clearly had no affection for Lorna Goodison. In fact, Tessa realised she had never heard anyone praise Lorna, all the time she had been at Foxleigh.

She felt she had to protest, weakly. 'She's a good-looking woman, though—lovely hair, and good clothes.'

'Clothes are no substitute for doing a poor job. Do you know, her surgery has to be over by six-thirty every evening? She has her bridge evenings over at the Manor, her Council work, and her Women's Institute, which she thinks will collapse without her guiding hand.'

Tessa couldn't help giggling. Straightening her face, she said, 'Joyce, you make yourself very clear.'

'Well, I'm sorry, but I can't stand a doctor who doesn't put her patients first, and that's a fact. And now I'd better shut up before I say something I shouldn't. Try your soup. I'll bet you'll be back here for more next week!'

They chatted of other things over the soup, which was every bit as good as promised. 'I am very glad I ran into you, Joyce.' Tessa stood up to go. 'See you on Monday.'

'I'm glad too. Look after yourself—and don't you be going around on your own, now. Come and see us whenever you're passing.' Joyce scribbled her address on a bit of paper. ''Bye now, Tessa.'

Tessa went back on the local bus, which stopped at the

hospital gates. On the way she pondered deeply about Lorna Goodison. The woman's name seemed to crop up wherever she went. She wasn't a witch, of that Tessa was sure, but it seemed almost as certain that she wasn't a very good GP either. Tessa tried to put it out of her mind. She knew that rumours were always blown up out of all proportion, especially in small communities like Foxleigh. She must be very fair, and believe nothing until it was proved.

That evening she went again to the dining-room. She was going to sit alone, but Dr Singh called her over, where he sat at a table for six with other juniors on call. 'Come and sit here, Dr Daley. We always sit here on a Saturday, in full view of the television set.'

'Thank you. But please call me Tessa.' She realised that she had been here almost two months, and had made no attempt to get to know the others well. She tried to make up for it by being chatty tonight. It was well worth the trouble. They were soon into a full-scale discussion about the present state of the nation's health, with touching contributions from Sandip Singh, who had spent some time in the poorer parts of rural India, and knew what real health problems were.

One of the housemen asked Tessa where she came from. 'I'm a Londoner, born and bred,' she told him.

'Ah, London.' Sandip was interested, his handsome dark eyes opening wide. 'Tell me, then, you must have been to the Wimbledon, and the Henley, and the Oval?' He spoke the names as though they were public houses.

Tessa laughed. 'Oh yes, I've done all that. And the Gold Cup.'

'You have been to the Ascot as well? You were wearing a big hat, yes?'

'Sandip, you don't have to look ridiculous to get into

Ascot, you know. If you must know, I wore a very tiny hat made of white feathers.' She smiled, as she remembered the year before last. 'But I didn't get any of the winners. And I didn't go last year . . .' Her voice faded, and she rose suddenly. 'I'll tell you more tomorrow.' Last year had been so dreadful. She didn't want to remember, not in front of all these strangers.

But Sandip walked to the door with her, and his voice was solemn. 'You are brave, coming in. It will be easier next time.'

'What do you mean?' she queried.

'I saw some tragedy in your face when I first met you. I am thankful that today you have come, and that you have laughed a little bit.'

Tessa looked into the lustrous black eyes, that returned her gaze sincerely. 'I thought—you would think me very stand-offish,' she explained.

He shook his head. 'I have never heard that phrase before, but I am sure that is not what we think.'

'Well, now I know I did the right thing, coming here.'

She was rewarded by his brilliant smile. 'I do hope you are going to the party, Tessa.'

'What party is this?' It sounded a bit too frivolous for her.

'Ah, you have not heard? Sir Harold's party. He gives one every year, so I am told, for the medical staff. You will probably find that your invitation is in your room. It is a dressy affair, they tell me. I hope you will attend.'

Tessa nodded. 'Well, I suppose if the Chief invites one, it would be impolite not to go. I'll be there, Sandip. Good night.'

When she got back to her quiet little flat, Tessa realised that the small buff envelope that Adam had delivered to her door that morning was in fact the invitation. 'Sir Harold and Lady Oliver . . . Dr T. Daley's company at a Reception and Buffet in the Great Hall.' She checked the date. She was on call, and would have to wear her bleep. Well, it was nice that Sir Harold wanted the pleasure of her company. She hadn't even spoken to him since she was appointed, and she still hadn't taken the trouble to go and watch him operate. She propped the card up on the bookcase, next to the *Bone and Joint Surgery* journal, the one with Adam's article in it.

Would Adam bring his beautiful Lorna? She would dress strikingly, something that would set off that glorious chestnut hair . . . With his athletic frame, he too would look pretty stunning in a dinner suit. Tessa frowned at herself. Now why did she allow herself to think that? Everyone looked good in a dinner suit. Little Sandip would look dapper. So would old Dr John, who had a paunch. And the blond anaesthetist, whom she had heard called 'Stringy' Shepherd, who was thin, and stooped. Why this sudden preoccupation with Adam Forrester's appearance? She forced herself to think of something else.

Sunday dawned grey and wet. Tessa heard the rain before she opened her eyes. She curled up, and tried to go back to sleep. But the previous happy day had started the adrenalin flowing into her system. She was beginning to come to life, like the reluctant hawthorns, showing their fresh new leaves in very gradual doses. She heard the church bells for early communion. They jarred her conscience. She had made use of the little church when she was miserable, so it seemed churlish to stay away now, just because it was raining.

She drank her morning tea, staring as usual out of her window. There were no skylarks today, no baby rabbits, and the grass was covered with the misty sheen of rain. She dressed in a tailored grey suit, and dug out her Burberry mackintosh to go over it. The wet pavements caused her to splash her tights. She had never bothered about that when she went around in old jeans, but never mind. The bells were ringing again, and she tramped the damp paths into the seventeenth-century church. The villagers were all there, the regulars, with their shapeless coats, their brilliantined hair. But now she knew several of them to speak to, and she nodded and smiled as she took her place, no longer a stranger.

When she made her way to the Brown Cow afterwards, there was a tall young man leaning across the bar, talking confidentially to Sam. Tessa hadn't seen him before, and he was outstandingly well dressed, in a perfectly cut suit and shoes you could see your face in, in spite of the rain. His must be the big Rover at the front, parked in such a way as to block the traffic going past through the village.

Tessa took her half pint, that Sam drew without being asked, over to her corner, where she could sit and decide whether she liked this new young man or not. He ordered a second double whisky, and splashed soda in carefully. He was a clean-cut type, with carefully trimmed hair, and the kind of horn-rimmed glasses that indicate the young executive. Was he just passing through? she wondered. Asking Sam the way?

The rain was becoming more steady, the sort of downpour that could go on for ever. But the snuggery was warm. Sam had a wood fire going, and its cheerful glow reflected on the horse brasses and copper buckets of trailing ferns and ivies. It was a typical English pub, warm, welcoming but discreet.

'Good morning, Tessa.'

A warm, velvet voice, one she recognised at once. 'Hello, Adam.' She didn't ask him to sit down, in case Lorna was just behind.

'May I?'

Tessa had already picked up her glass, expecting him to have gone. 'I'm sorry—of course you may. I thought you'd be meeting Lorna.' She made room for him to sit down, and fussed over his damp jacket. 'You're very wet. Didn't you come by car?'

'No. The rain wasn't too heavy when I left the hospital.' He brushed his sleeves a couple of times, and shook back his damp dark locks. 'What are you drinking?'

'Nothing, thanks.' She touched the glass before her.

He ordered a beer for himself and brought it back to the table. 'I wanted to have a word, Tessa—about Lorna. What do you really know about her?'

'That's a funny question. I know very little. I've only spoken to her once.'

'I wondered why—why you mentioned Mother Crowe the other night.'

'I was only teasing. I'd just come past her cottage, and had a word with Billy Blackshaw, so it was still in my mind, that's all.'

He took a deep breath. Then he sipped his beer and took another breath before saying slowly, 'Then I'm very sorry, I was rude. I thought you were trying to be smart—I ought to know you better by now. You didn't know that Mother Crowe's son is suing Lorna for malpractice?'

'Oh, my goodness!' Tessa put her hands to her mouth.

Adam bent his head lower. 'That's him at the bar. I bet he's trying to get some dirt on Lorna from Sam.'

Tessa didn't say anything to that. She knew very well that Sam had no time for either Lorna or Adam, but whether he would tell tales or not, she didn't know. She was inclined to think that Sam would be too canny to get himself involved in anything.

'The Defence Union are looking after it, of course,' Adam said. 'But I feel I ought to be doing something to help her.'

'Is there anything I can do?' Tessa had to say it, though she was reluctant.

'Don't listen to gossip, Tessa, that's all. Jack Crowe is going round trying to find people who are willing to talk—you know the sort of story—wrong medicine, not examining properly, serious conditions not diagnosed in time, that sort of thing. It can't be proved, and he's wasting his time. But he wants to blacken Lorna's name in any way he can.'

'But why, Adam? Last time I saw Mother Crowe, she was fine.'

He looked at her incredulously. 'You haven't heard?'

'I'm not exactly a chatty person, Adam.'

'No, fair enough.' He drank his beer in silence for a while. Neither of them spoke. Then he said, 'Mother Crowe's got inoperable cancer. Jack is saying that his mother went to Lorna last year with pains in her stomach. They only found out when they operated, and found they had to remove the pancreas. But the liver and spleen are involved as well, so there's no hope.'

Tessa swallowed and said carefully, 'That's a difficult one to diagnose, even for the experts.'

Adam nodded, looking into his empty glass as though trying to read his fortune. 'Yes, sure. But there are biochemical tests she could have arranged. Not that it would have saved Mother Crowe, but at least they would have been spared this shock.' He stopped himself, and went on quickly, 'Not that I'm sticking up for Lorna, but

I feel this sort of witch-hunt achieves nothing.' And the mention of witches made them both think of Billy Blackshaw and his preoccupation with the evil eye. It wasn't a very comfortable thought.

Tessa saw in Adam's face what he must be going through. Lorna must be depending on him for support, and the more he heard, the more he must realise that Jack Crowe did have a basis for a case. She said quickly, 'It's a bad business, Adam, but you can count on me. I'll be all three wise monkeys rolled into one!' She tried not to think of Harry Ramsbotham. Lorna Goodison would have received Tessa's letter by now, making it clear that she, too, had caught Lorna out in a serious mistake. Lorna would know that Tessa was in a position to add to the cases against her.

She would have liked to talk frankly to Adam, to tell him what Joyce Ainsley had said. It was common knowledge that Lorna finished surgery quickly in the evenings, because of her golf and her bridge, her Council work and WI. Yet Tessa knew doctors who had many interests, and still ran a good practice. Had Lorna just been unlucky? And if this business blew over, would it have taught her a lesson? Perhaps it was a good thing that she had been found out before any more serious harm was done . . .

Jack Crowe was leaving, shaking hands with Sam. Did that mean he'd been of help? They all heard the sound of his car engine start up, as he drove the few yards down the road to his mother's now empty cottage. She must be in Blackwood Infirmary. Tessa was still staring at the pelting rain outside, when there was a stir among the locals in the bar. Lorna Goodison was coming in. She must have waited until Jack Crowe had left, seen him drive away.

Lorna, as always, looked like an advertisement out of *Country Life*. She closed her slim umbrella and shook back her immaculate chestnut bob, showing the glitter of diamonds in her ears. She was wearing a dog-tooth check jacket over a brown pleated skirt. Her country brogues were the type for sitting in pubs, rather than hiking over the fields. She raked the room with her narrowed green eyes, and saw Adam. She took a step towards him, then she saw Tessa, and her face worked. She glared.

She said in a voice hoarse with anger, 'So she's got at you now! That's me finished!' And she turned on her heel and rushed out into the driving rain.

Adam stood up. 'I'll have to go. She needs me.'

CHAPTER FOUR

TESSA tried not to listen to the inevitable gossip about Lorna Goodison. She had met the woman by chance, and she also had personal experience of her carelessness at work. And now she was at the receiving end of Lorna's bitter dislike—surely she could not be jealous of Tessa having the odd drink with Adam? It didn't make sense. But the atmosphere between the two women was none of Tessa's making, and whenever Lorna's name was mentioned, Tessa made a point of ignoring it. Meanwhile, the grey landscape turned very slowly to green as she worked.

She had not spoken to Adam for a week. He was always in a rush, either going or coming, when she went to the dining-room. She wondered how much Lorna's troubles were affecting him, but she said nothing. She just hoped that Mother Crowe's son would not start his investigations in the hospital. 'He's been in touch with the head of Action for the Victims of Medical Accidents, you know,' Joyce Ainsley had told Tessa.

And Tessa had smiled, and moved on to do her ward round, making it clear that the subject was taboo. But it all sounded as though Jack Crowe meant to make things as nasty as possible for Dr Lorna Goodison.

When Saturday came, Tessa was feeling low again. She must not expect any dramatic improvement, she knew. But things had weighed less heavily on her mind recently, and she had hoped she was getting over Guy. But she had dreamed of him last night. True, it was only in passing; he had just been one of a group of faces that had appeared to her in a jumbled way. But when she woke, she had the feeling that he was still with her, and it was a shock to have to tell herself that there was nothing left of Guy Trethowan but her own memories.

She was reluctant to get up. There was a feeble sun trying to shine, but there was no heat in the pale rays. She lay staring at the sky, feeling the heaviness of her heart, and the hopelessness of any happiness in her future.

The front doorbell rang, and she started up, feeling ashamed of being caught in bed. Her mother's words came back to her, words about girls being idle, and 'slovenly actions made slovenly minds.' Dear Mum! She had worked so hard, being both mother and father to the growing Tessa, that she had worn herself out. She had died when Tessa was in her first year at university. At least she had seen Tessa do well in her first exams, and she knew her dear daughter would be a doctor. Tessa decided she must copy her mother more. She had coped on her own, and she had never grumbled about it—not once.

Tessa swung herself out of bed and grabbed her housecoat. She opened the door an inch, and there was Adam Forrester, with his dark blue gaze, smiling down at her. She was acutely conscious of her tousled hair and bleary eyes. 'Oh, Adam—' she began.

His voice was hearty. 'Good morning, neighbour. Late night last night, eh? May I come in?' He was upright and handsome in jeans and a sweatshirt.

Tessa opened the door wider. 'Yes, of course. Will you have some coffee?'

'Why don't I make it, while you get into some clothes? I was hoping very much that you'd come for a long walk with me.' Tessa's heart began to thump. She ought to be ashamed of it, but she knew she did want to accept his invitation. Only—ought she? He said, 'Would you like to, Tess? I'm very selfish, I know. But—well, I've had my ear chewed off all week, and you are a nice quiet companion. You said yourself that you weren't exactly the chatty type, and that's just the type I'd love to spend a day with. If you'll have me.'

Tessa laughed. How could she refuse such a down-to-earth invitation? If he'd said it any other way, she might have been afraid—afraid of becoming too involved with him. But as she was only asked because she didn't chatter, that suited her very well. She said, equally frankly, 'Well, I'd like to, Adam. But I'm not the athletic type as well, you know, and I doubt if I could keep up with you.'

He was already in the kitchen, rattling cups and saucers as he took them from the cupboard. 'I promise not to go over twenty miles an hour.'

'Then it's a date.' She quickly turned on the shower and scrubbed herself vigorously. She had no need to ask who it was who had been chewing his ear off. It was Lorna, desperately clinging to him, relying on him for moral support in her troubles. And Tessa felt a certain warmth, that he had come to her for relief and relaxation. That's what real friends were for. But friends—nothing more than friends; of that she was determined.

As she put on a shirt and jeans, she smelt toast and butter as well as coffee. She usually didn't bother with breakfast, but she was suddenly hungry, and glad of the food. 'Thank you, Adam. It's good of you.'

'Not really. I don't want you flaking out on me because of a low blood sugar.' He laughed at her expression. 'No, I promise faithfully not to exhaust you. I just felt a good blow in the fresh air would do both of us some good.' And she noticed that his face did look more careworn than usual. His brow was creased with tension, and there were fine lines in the skin at the corners of his deep blue eyes.

Tessa cleaned her teeth and gave her hair a good brush. She had half thought of looking for a hairdresser in Blackwood this morning, but that could wait. With the brushing, she thought that maybe there was just a hint of the original healthy colour coming back, a trace of the sheen it once had. 'I'm ready,' she told him.

'Well done! Some women would have taken hours.' Neither of them said it, but she knew he meant Lorna again. That exquisite make-up must take some time to apply.

She merely said, 'They would probably look nicer than I do.'

'Not really.' Adam's voice was carefully neutral, but she felt an electric thrill inside her at the implied compliment. He opened the door for her, and she could sense the heat of his body as she passed him. They ran down the stairs together. 'My car's over there, under the oak,' he said.

She had seen him occasionally driving this sleek silver BMW, but she had seen him more often in the shiny white Porsche. Again she wondered if Sam Browne was right, if Adam Forrester was pursuing his association with Lorna just because she was rich, and her father was in a position to help him in his career . . . Still, it didn't matter today.

He opened the door for her, and she sat in the passenger seat, looking up at the branches of the oak tree, gnarled and still bare, the anaemic sun casting intermittent shadows on the metallic finish of the car. 'Where are we going?' she asked.

'Pennines. Get some real fresh air along those lazy airways.'

'The Pennines? Is it far?'

'Depends how fast you drive,' he said, with a quiet grin. Tessa looked at him as he started the engine. This must be the first time she had sat in a car with a man since . . . Adam's profile was very handsome, and she didn't miss Guy at that moment. She was hoping she would not begin to like this man too much. He was growing in attractiveness all the time, and that would not do. It would be unfaithful and wrong—especially as he was 'on the make' and made no secret of the fact that he was going to the States soon. He was perfect for an acquaintance, the occasional day out, but nothing more. Tessa was on her guard.

Adam was right—it didn't seem far to the Derbyshire hills, along leafy Cheshire lanes winding between fresh green country. Then the gentle plain gave way to rugged uplands. They left the little grey towns behind, and were soon among wild rolling hills and moors, covered with tough brown scrub. There were hardly any trees, only flinty walls, greyish sheep, and tiny white lambs. Again Tessa saw Adam as Heathcliff, looking rugged and tough against this harsh open backcloth.

'What are you thinking?' he queried suddenly. They were climbing, and the car whined upwards in second gear.

She blushed. One doesn't tell a man he looks like a Brontë hero. 'It's really nice of you to bring me,' she prevaricated.

'Damn it, woman, it's nice of you to put up with me and my moods.' He smiled at her, with a sidelong glance from his steering. 'I still don't know you very well, Dr Daley, but what I do know, I happen to like a lot. You're the kind of person I feel at home with, Tess. You make me feel calm and—well—good.'

Tessa could say nothing. She wanted to tell him she felt the same, but it smacked too much of getting too familiar. After a short silence, broken only by the purr of the engine, she said, 'When I saw you that Sunday in Foxleigh Church, I thought you looked terribly sad. Yet you aren't a sad person at all, are you?'

He stole another look at her before turning his attention back to the winding road. 'No, just bad-tempered. And that day I was feeling rather frustrated—by the Health Service, and by a private thing between me and Sir Harold.'

She didn't pry; he had said it was private. 'So you thought you would solve your problems by emigrating. Have you made your mind up yet?'

'No.' And she wondered if this business with Lorna Goodison was preventing him from making plans. He wasn't the sort of man to run out on someone if she needed him. Not to mention keeping well in with the family . . . Tessa looked out at the rolling moorland. She didn't like people who kowtowed to rich and powerful people, but Adam didn't strike her at that type. Yet she knew so little about him. And, in his words, what she saw, she liked a lot.

They had reached a fairly level stretch of road, and Adam swung the car into a narrow side road, between drystone walls. 'We'll leave the car along here, then we can make a circular walk,' he told her.

'How many miles?'

He smiled at her, and immediately she stopped worrying. 'Not too far—I did promise.' He stopped the car in a gateway, obviously unused, tied up with string and rusty wire. 'There. Now, out you get, love, and breathe in. Let's get some roses into those cheeks.'

She obeyed. The air was fresh, and she caught her breath in its cheeky attacks. She grabbed her anorak and closed the door. 'I'm ready. Which way?'

'Follow me.' He locked the car and vaulted lightly over a stile. Then he turned to help Tessa over. 'What do you think?'

She gazed out across a vast expanse of bleak moorlands. 'Does it ever get green?'

'Oh yes, when the new bracken comes through. We'll come again in a few weeks, and you'll see the difference.' For some reason she felt glad. Adam had confirmed that their relationship was safe for the next few weeks. And again she had to warn herself she must not become dependent on this charming but unreliable young surgeon. She could not bear to be hurt again; she must stay on her guard with Adam Forrester.

They walked lightly across springy turf and moss, and the air felt pure and wholesome. 'I feel as though I haven't been breathing at all for the last month!' exclaimed Tessa. They stepped out across the moors, and she felt the exhilaration of her own good health. She wondered what it must be like to be Sharon Billington, never to feel this good, never to be able to stride out and walk, never to put back her shoulders, and rejoice in the ability of her own body. It must be dreadful to be young, and to be trapped in a twisted and feeble body. Yet Sharon had never complained. Only her pale face had shown the frustration and desolation that she felt— followed by the noble look of resignation and cheerfulness that she assumed when her young husband came to collect her.

'Want a rest?' She had not been going to ask, but she was glad of the chance to sit on a low wall, and catch her breath.

'Out of condition,' she smiled.

'And too proud to admit it.' Adam looked at her intently, and she found herself blushing and lowering her gaze. 'Why won't you look at me, Tessa?'

She allowed herself to look at him, let him see the reddening of her cheeks at his closeness. She knew he could read her face then, and that it was plain that she did find him attractive. He bent suddenly, and his lips brushed against her cheek. Then she was in his arms, and he was kissing her on the lips, hard and sweet and intoxicating.

But he felt the tears on her cheeks, and drew away. Neither of them spoke for a while, just stood close together, her head touching his shoulder. Her tears continued to fall, silently. Adam looked out, as though unseeing, across the dull, harsh brown hills. 'Do you want to tell me? What's his name?'

'Guy.' It was too late; they had crossed that border between friendship and attachment. There was no point in hiding anything now. 'He was a pilot—he was killed in a flying accident.'

'I'm sorry, I had no idea—How long ago?'

'Last summer.'

'I see.' And she knew he did see. There was no need to explain any more. He saw why she had come to Fox-leigh, why she didn't bother with clothes or make-up, why she wanted to be left alone with her work. And she was suddenly glad she had told him. Adam was the only person she had told, and he would now respect her wish for solitude. And she knew he wouldn't give her secret away, unless she gave him permission.

He had too much integrity.

He stood up. 'Ready?' She nodded, and they set off again, across a small sloping field. There was a burst of cold wind, and Tessa shivered. Adam put his hand lightly on her shoulder, and they walked together, her heart growing calmer, her feelings strangely happy.

There was a small stone building across the field; she thought it was a barn. But as they approached, she saw it was an inn, standing lonely and windswept on the road that was little more than a sheep track. 'Lunchtime,' said Adam, leading the way down some poorly lit steps. Tessa was surprised to find the little snuggery quite full of hikers, in anoraks and big boots. Adam ordered two large Scotches, and a plate of roast beef sandwiches. They ate in companionable silence, after Adam had explained where they were, and why the inn was there. 'We're not far from the famous Goyt Valley,' he explained.

She nodded. 'Yes, I've heard of it—thyroid country.' She said casually, 'I suppose in the old days they would blame witchcraft for the over-active thyroids, wouldn't they?'

'Have you been talking to Billy Blackshaw again?' He seemed disinclined to talk about witches, and Tessa sipped her whisky, and felt the chill disappear from her limbs. But she ought not to have mentioned witches. Lorna must have been very upset, to know that she was accused of putting an evil eye on anyone. Tessa had been long enough in the country to realise that some customs are long remembered.

They walked back, refreshed. The conversation was superficial now, they spoke only of impersonal things, but Tessa felt safer that way. Yet she had the feeling that

Adam had hoped he could confide in her a little, and was now backing off.

The walk was more than Tessa was used to, and she fell asleep in the car on the way back. When she jerked awake, it was as they were turning into the hospital drive, and there had been a sudden and ill-mannered hoot of an expensive horn. Lorna. The white Porsche pulled away on the main road, and Tessa sat up, rubbing her eyes, and looked after it. Adam did nothing, keeping his eyes coolly on the drive and steering neatly into his place in the staff car park. 'She came to see you?' Tessa queried.

He smiled. 'Probably. She doesn't go a bundle on visiting patients, especially now.'

He didn't sound worried. Tessa said, 'You should go after her, Adam. She might be in trouble.'

He raised his eyebrows as he switched off the engine. 'Before having a hot bath and a shave? I daren't!' He was teasing, but she saw a tension start up in him, that had been absent all day until now. 'I'll call her later.'

Tessa said softly, 'It's been a wonderful day—all of it, every minute.'

'And for me.' He looked into her face for a moment. He was smiling, but she saw the worry behind his eyes, the nervous twitch of the lips. Impulsively, Tessa leaned over and touched his cheek with her mouth, very softly. Then she opened the door and ran upstairs without looking back. She didn't hear him get out of the car until she was in her room, and flopped down on the sofa, her mind in a turmoil of bad and good vibrations. As she heard the car door slam, and gentle noises in the flat below, the good vibrations took over. He was a good man. How could he be what Sam Browne said he was? Surely if he'd been a pushy, selfish sort of person, it would have shown today. They had been together for almost twelve hours, and not once had there been disharmony.

She stretched out, arching her back, and knowing that tomorrow she would discover muscles that had stayed hidden for many months. But it had been fun, and Adam Forrester was a good neighbour. She was lucky to have a friend like him, who would ask no more of her than friendship. She was like a—like a maiden aunt! He could bring his troubles to her, and know he had a sympathetic ear for his woes. She smiled. What would Adam say if she told him she was his maiden aunt? Just for a moment, she felt the searing strength of his kiss that afternoon—but it was a passion soon leashed, and one that she knew he would redirect towards Lorna, the woman who needed him so much.

She gave the dining-room a miss and drove down to the Brown Cow for a snack. Sam Browne was busy, but she saw him looking at the door, saw the expression of relief when she came in. Had he been waiting for her? She had made no promises. In fact, she resented anything that made her feel tied down; she wanted to be free to make her own decisions, and Sam was getting a little too domineering towards her. Yet she was touched by his affection, and gave him a cheerful smile as she sat down with her fried chicken and salad. He gave a little wave, which meant that he would get over to speak when he had the chance.

'Tessa, you look stunning.' The rush had died down, and Sam came over to talk, leaving Annie and Sarah Blunt to mind the bar, the two old sisters from next door to the Post Office. Tessa knew almost everyone in the village by now.

'That's kind of you. I just thought I'd wear a dress

instead of those endless jeans.'

'And very sweet you look. You must let me buy you a drink.'

'No, Sam.' Tessa was firm. 'We can't be friends if you say things like that. Anyway, I had a large drink at lunchtime. We went up to Derbyshire—it was really fun.'

Sam's face fell. He didn't ask who 'we' were; he obviously knew. Tessa did her best to sparkle, describing herself lagging behind, and getting as breathless as an old woman.

'Talking of old women, I hear Mother Crowe is in a coma,' said Sam.

Tessa looked grave. 'I'm sorry. But she is over eighty, isn't she? Even the best of sons couldn't expect his mother to live for ever. It's all for the best, if she slips away without any more pain.'

Sam nodded into his beard. 'You're right, and I agree with you. But Jack has a bee in his bonnet about Dr Goodison. He seems determined to bring some kind of lawsuit against her. You know he was pumping me last Sunday?'

'Yes, I did see. He was talking to you a long time.'

'I wasn't going to repeat any gossip, but things are looking black. The cases are piling up, as far as I could judge.'

'We ought to stay out of it, Sam,' said Tessa anxiously.

'Too right. But I can't help hearing things in here, and believe me, there's many a one more than willing to tell their own tale of woe. Lorna isn't well liked, and that's a fact. She's going to need everything her daddy can do for her—and more.' And she's going to need Adam Forrester as well, Tessa thought to herself. And she pretended that she was glad that poor Lorna had his support and love. But secretly, she felt a little pang of—was it annoyance, or anger? That Lorna was lucky enough to have Adam at her beck and call. He was too good for her. Unless Sam was right, and Adam was keeping well in with the family merely for his own ambitious reasons.

Sam said, 'So what else have you been doing, apart from marathon fell-walking? Still enjoying the work at Foxleigh?'

'Yes, I am. I like the patients, and I'm impressed by the surgical team. They're world authorities, some of them. I'm hoping to watch Sir Harold operate next week. And Adam Forrester had an excellent article in the *Journal* this week.'

'Ah, Tricky Dicky is still at work capturing all hearts, is he?'

'Sam, that was hardly fair!' Tessa wondered at the vehemence of Sam's comment.

'Okay, maybe it wasn't, but he's sticking his neck out for Lorna Goodison against Mother Crowe's son, isn't he, and that's not very ethical, Tessa, not from where I'm standing. Because I believe there's no smoke without fire, and a lot of those stories must have a grain of truth in them.'

'No, Sam, not necessarily. You don't know medicine. It's not easy to be right all the time. There must be lots of doctors who get away with mistakes because they're nice people, and their patients like them. Poor Lorna isn't very popular, so it's much easier to get patients to grumble. We doctors are used to being grumbled at —it's all part of the job, really.'

He stood up at once. 'I didn't mean to offend you, Tessa. I was only speaking my mind—it's a habit folk have around here.' He turned again. 'I didn't want to spoil anything between us, I've sent for the Hallé Orchestra's syllabus. I thought maybe you'd come to a concert with me next month?'

His expression reminded her again of the open devotion of his own red setter. Her spirited reply had obviously made him think he had lost her regard. She said, 'That would be nice.' But there wasn't as much warmth in her tone as she intended. His jealousy of Adam Forrester had annoyed her. Because surely there was no basis for it? To Tessa, Adam was only a colleague and a friend. There was nothing at all to be jealous of . . .

She drove back to the hospital. But a vivid white moon had come out, and the sky was studded with stars. She passed the hospital entrance, deciding to take a longer way back, to enjoy the beauty of the evening—and to allow her irritation with Sam Browne to dissipate in the wider environment of the moonlit hedges and fields.

There was a small farmhouse on one corner, with a lorry in the drive, and a large van parked outside. She had to slow up, to make sure there was no traffic in the opposite direction. 'Dr Daley, what are you doing out this way?' She turned in surprise and looked through her open window.

There was a young couple, arms linked, just turning into the farm, which she saw was called 'Grant's Farm' in white letters on the gate. Of course, that was Sharon Billington's address. 'Hello, Sharon. How nice to see you out and about.'

Sharon was small and well built, though her legs were thin, as the muscles wasted beneath swollen knees. She pulled her young husband to meet Tessa. 'How do you do,' said Tessa. 'We're going to meet at next week's clinic, aren't we, to try and get on top of this arthritis, before it gets on top of us.' She spoke heartily. She didn't want poor Sharon to give up. It was important that they all kept a fighting spirit.

'That's right.' Kenneth Billington reached out, and shook Tessa's hand. But his voice was sullen, and her heart sank, as she had expected him to be more co-operative.

'You'll be able to come? If it's difficult, I'll pop out and see you at home some time.'

'I'll come all right, Doctor.' But his tone had worsened. 'But it's that Dr Goodison I'm annoyed with. Sharon had this trouble for over a year, and she never did a damn thing about it. I'm certain that's why she's that bad now.'

CHAPTER FIVE

THAT afternoon's clinic was the first Tessa had ever held when only seven-eighths of her attention was devoted to her work. The other part was worrying about Lorna Goodison, and worrying seriously. There was no doubt now that Lorna was indeed failing in her duty as a doctor: both Harry Ramsbotham and Sharon Billington were examples of careless diagnosis. Was Lorna careless? Or was she just in a hurry, because of all her other interests? Whatever the reason, Tessa was on the side of the patients. But though she knew something must be said, she hesitated about who to speak to.

The fairest thing would be to confront Lorna head-on. She might resent it, but things could not be allowed to go on like this. Alternatively, she could have a word with Dr Blake, Lorna's senior partner. But she did not know him, and she did not want to worry him unnecessarily. Perhaps the best thing would be to speak to Adam Forrester. After all, he had mentioned it to Tessa, when he asked her to stay out of the whole business. In all honour, she could not stay out now, knowing what she knew. She would ask Adam. If he advised her to speak to Lorna, they could do it together.

'Dr Daley?' Tessa looked up at her next patient with a start.

'Sorry, Sharon.' It was Sharon Billington, with her husband beside her. He was a curly-headed young man, with a boyish face. She would have expected him to be full of fun, but his eyes were serious today. He had taken on more than most men of his age, and he seemed intent on making a success of it.

Tessa reached for Sharon's file and took out the latest blood test results. 'Yes, Sharon. I'm glad you both came, Kenneth. I think we ought to discuss the long-term prospects with you—that is, as far as we can without the aid of a crystal ball.'

'Dr Daley—' Sharon held up a hand, and her face showed a mixture of fear and happiness. Poor girl! Most girls in the first flush of marriage showed only happiness. 'I saw Dr Goodison a couple of days ago, and she sent me for a pregnancy test. They told us this morning that it was positive.'

Tessa was used to thinking quickly. She knew very well that the eyes of the young couple were on her, and that any dismay she showed would upset them very much. Pregnancy—with such active disease—it could mean trouble. On the other hand, it might be perfectly normal. In this situation, there was only one thing to say. She smiled . 'Well, congratulations to you both.'

Kenneth said gravely, 'Then you don't think—? It isn't a bad thing, then?'

'A bad thing for a happily married couple to have a baby? Certainly not.' She saw that the shadow was not yet quite gone from Sharon's face. 'I know what you're thinking—you're likely to have extra difficulties. Your hands—they're all right at the moment?' She saw that the fingers were swollen, but the joints themselves were relatively normal, not knotted or bent in dislocation.

'They've been fine since Mr Forrester saw me. He gave me some injections.'

'Good. Then there's no reason why they shouldn't stay fine for some time. Pregnancy works in a funny way, Sharon. You may find that all your pain and stiffness goes away for a while. But you must be prepared for it to come back at some stage. It may not—I just don't want you to get too depressed if it does. There's an awful lot we can do these days. Many patients lead an absolutely normal life.' She turned to Kenneth. 'You're pleased about the baby?'

'Oh yes.' His face had cleared. 'I did want a family. So long as Sharon's going to be okay.'

'We'll look after her, I promise. And I see from your notes that you both have parents and relatives close by. I'm sure they'll rally round, won't they?'

'You bet!' Sharon and Kenneth smiled at each other.

Tessa perused her notes. She was glad, in a way, that this decision had been taken out of her hands. If they had asked for her opinion before starting a baby, she would have had to point out the disadvantages. As it was, she would support them wholeheartedly. Kenneth Billington said, 'You know, Doctor, I was afraid you might tell her she had to—well—get rid of the baby.'

Tessa shook her head. 'Never. And with parents like you? That little one is lucky, and will bring you lots of fun.'

Sharon leaned back, relaxed at last. 'Is there anything special I need to do?'

'Well, yes, I'll need to review your drug therapy at once. Less cortisone, of course—the fewer drugs you take the better. But as I expect you to be feeling well, you won't need them. Lots of rest—at least a couple of hours every afternoon—but a few healthy walks in the fresh air too. So long as you don't put too much strain on your knees. Take them when you feel at your best—and sensible shoes, of course.'

'What about iron tablets, Doctor? My sister had to take iron tablets for the whole nine months.'

Tessa nodded. 'When you've been booked in at Blackwood Maternity, Sharon, let me have the name of the consultant who's looking after you. I'll write to him about your present therapy, and we'll decide about the iron together. Sometimes it doesn't agree with arthritics.'

Sharon and her husband stood up. 'You've been so kind, taking the trouble to explain so clearly. If it's a girl, Dr Daley, I'd like to call her after you.'

Tessa felt a little jerk at her heart at their appreciation. She had done nothing more than her job. Except, of course, that she had not shown her apprehension at the pregnancy. Yet to them it was so much. She had been honest—yet made sure that they both looked forward to the future. Kenneth put his arm around his limping wife as they walked out. Even with rheumatoid arthritis, Sharon Billington had more to look forward to than a healthy but empty-hearted Tessa Daley.

She saw Adam Forrester in the dining-room that evening. But he only waved a hand and strode across to join Mr Shepherd, where they both bent their heads over a sheaf of notes. She would try and catch him later. He clearly would not welcome a chat about Lorna's misdeeds at the moment. Tessa ate alone, then went into the lounge, where Sandip Singh was watching television.

'Come and tell me more stories about the glamour of London society?' he invited.

She laughed. 'It—well, it was fun. But overrated.'

He said quietly, 'You had many friends there? Maybe a boy-friend?'

'I did know quite a lot of people.' She knew that Sandip had noted her depression when she first arrived, and had put two and two together. But she was unwilling

to open her heart too much; she didn't want to go over
the past.

'They would not, perhaps, enjoy the life at Foxleigh?
Very slow, isn't it? Not much of the bright lights?'

'You're right,' she smiled. 'Clubs, dancing, theatres
—I don't think there was anyone much struck on country life.' She thought of Gloria's phrase. 'They thought I
was going up among the slagheaps! It just shows how
wrong people can be.' She had seen not a single slagheap
in this part of rural Lancashire, only flat fields and rolling
moorland. And the little things that had given her
pleasure—the baby rabbits, the skylark's song, the dapper black and white of the fluttering magpies. Her
London crowd would not have looked twice at them.

'Telephone for you, Dr Daley.' She had heard the
ring, but she was not on call, and had ignored the shrill
summons. She took the receiver from the lounge wall-
set. Did one of the wards want her?

'Tessa, is that you?'

'Yes. Hello, Sam.' She recognised the velvety voice.

'I was just wondering—if you were all right. You
weren't in yesterday. I was hoping you might pop down
to see us tonight.'

She recognised the loneliness in his voice, and it was a
warning. She didn't want him to make any demands on
her. She must not allow him to make her feel guilty for
not going down to see him regularly. She must make it
clear that he was only a friend—like Sandip, or Adam
Forrester. 'I've been busy, Sam. Was there anything
special you wanted to talk about?'

'No, love. I just missed your quiet little body, and
hoped you were all right.'

There it was again, the hangdog tone of a lonely man
who wanted a shoulder to lean on. 'I'm fine, thanks,

Sam. Just tired.' She rang off as soon as she could. 'See you some time, Sam. Thanks for calling.'

She stood for a moment by the phone. Everyone was sitting watching television, or reading. Tessa decided she was tired, and made her way quietly to the door.

She was conscious of the hush in the hospital as she walked slowly along the corridor, and out through the side door towards the doctors' flats, only a few yards away. The night was dark, clouds hiding the moon. The air was chill, although it was almost officially spring. She clasped her arms across her chest, feeling the cold as she climbed the stairs.

Adam's door was ajar, and she heard a movement inside. Perhaps now was a good time to have a word about Lorna. She tapped lightly on the door. 'Adam?'

He came at once. He was wearing a pale blue pullover and blue jeans. 'That's a nice surprise—the first time you've ever wanted to talk to me!'

'You won't think it's nice when I tell you why I've come.'

He looked down at her, and she again felt the force of his good looks. Those eyes were so expressive, slightly amused, but with a touch of gravity. A girl could easily lose herself in the intensity of Adam's full attention —and many probably had . . . 'Come and sit down. Tell me all. You were deep in conversation with Sandy Singh earlier, so I didn't intrude.'

'Oh, that,' Tessa smiled. 'He seemed fascinated by London life.'

As she entered, he gave a little laugh. 'He would have been fascinated if you gave him a history of refuse collection in darkest Wigan! Don't you see? They're all keen to get to know the loveliest creature to hit Foxleigh since the days of Florence Weatherall—but that's

another story altogether.' He followed her into the
lounge. 'They're all dying for you to stop and chat. John
Finch thinks you're the best-looking woman doctor he's
ever met, Shepherd can't wait to get to know you better,
and Sandy Singh has already asked me if I thought you'd
accept if he invited you out. Can't you see that much,
Tess?'

She sat down, rather bewildered. She liked the
way he—and only he—shortened her name. Tess. It
sounded so nice, the way he said it. She could think of
nothing to say, except, 'Who is Florence Weatherall?'

He sat beside her on the sofa. 'She was a dark-eyed
beauty of a physiotherapist, who had all hearts a-flutter
about three years ago. She worked her way through the
medical and surgical staff, as I recall. There were bets
taken as to whom she would choose in the end.'

Tessa said, 'And—?'

'She married a wealthy patient with an artificial hip,
and they went to live on his yacht in the South of France.'
He was smiling, and Tessa smiled back, feeling again
that she got on well with this man. Even if he had been
out with Florence Weatherall . . . He made her feel
comfortable—except when he made her feel physically
attracted to him, which frightened her a little.

'Well, I'm a bit ordinary to be in Florence's category,
then.'

He said in a low voice, 'Don't tell me that Guy of yours
never told you how beautiful you were?'

She felt a little shiver down her spine. 'Well, yes, quite
often. But in those days I was trying hard. I used to like
clothes, and dressing up to the nines, and I had my hair
done in the Kings Road every week. And I—well, I was
happy . . .'

'And now you're not happy, and you're not trying

hard.' He moved an inch or two nearer to her. 'And you're still gorgeous. See?' He lowered his voice and whispered, 'Why do you think I left my door open?'

'You're teasing me!'

He stood up, and looked down at her. 'Yes, I'm only teasing—I think.' She looked up at him, trying to read his face. He murmured, his voice getting husky, 'But don't stare at me with those big green eyes or I might forget.'

She looked down, and said crossly, 'Adam, please be serious. And my eyes are blue. I want to talk to you about Lorna Goodison.'

'Fair enough—they're greeny-blue.' He sat down, this time in the chair opposite to her. 'Fire away. What about Lorna?'

Tessa told him the full story of her two patients, and his face grew grave. 'So you see, I don't want to be bitchy, but it's either negligence or ignorance. We have to think of the patients. If she can't give them better treatment, then something's badly wrong. This case Mother Crowe's son is bringing—might be the only thing that will make her think twice about what she's doing.'

Adam began to pace up and down over the slightly worn carpet. 'Damn the woman!' His voice was low, as he muttered to himself. 'How did I ever get into this?' His face had taken on the rather hunted look that Tessa had noticed that first day in church. It was obvious that his love for the beautiful Lorna was more of a worry than a pleasure to him at present. He turned to Tessa. 'Help me, Tess. You decide what's best.'

Her heart went out to him. 'But I came for your advice.'

'Okay. Hang on while I get us some coffee, and we'll

put our heads together.' He went into the little kitchen. 'Black or white?' She heard the sound of a filter coffee-maker hissing and bubbling.

'White, please. I need my sleep.'

He put his head round the door. 'I suppose it's no use telling you what I need?'

She faced his look squarely, but she felt a blush creep up over her cheeks. She understood him well enough —and he saw that she did. Only the ceasing of the hissing of the coffee-maker made him turn away from her, in order to pour out two china mugs of coffee. It was with relief to Tessa that the compelling figure in his blue sweater and jeans disappeared from her view for a moment or two. She quickly moved from the sofa to a chair, so that there was no danger of him sitting too close to her for her peace of mind.

But even that move was noticed, and his eyes were amused as he handed her the coffee. But he did not tease her any further. 'Well, have you had time to think what we should do? About Lorna, I mean.'

She sipped the warm liquid, gathering her composure. 'One of us must tell her, that we know she isn't doing her job properly. Gosh, it's not an easy thing to tell anyone, least of all someone medical. But she has to know. I can't keep quiet if I'm asked. I have proof of her inefficiency.'

'Yes, I see that.' Adam looked down, miserably, at the mug he held between his two hands. 'To be honest, I feel you ought to speak to her. After all, you're the one who's picked up these two mistakes. The only thing is—I feel a bit of a blighter to ask you to do it, because I know she can be very nasty to you.'

Tessa smiled a little. 'You don't know me, Adam. I can be fairly nasty too, if I try. We must only hope it won't be necessary.'

'Then you don't mind?'

'No. I only wanted to make sure you knew. It was you who asked me to stay out of the affair.' She put down her mug. 'So I have your approval?'

'You have it.' They exchanged glances again, and she saw that the twinkle had come back to his eyes. 'All of it.'

Tessa picked up her mug again, to hide her confusion. She could think of no quick rejoinder to his implied compliment. In truth, she had to admit to herself that she found pleasure in his approval, and in his open admission of it. If only she had met this man before Guy, and that he was not tied up so willingly to Lorna. But even if she were free of her loyalty to Guy, Adam would not be free. They could flirt a little, quite safely, enjoy their little jokes together, their easy conversations—because they both knew that it could go no further. Neither of them was free to follow up idle dreams, attractive though they were.

It was time to go, and she stood up. 'Right, I'll do it. Shall I ring Lorna at her surgery?'

'No, better not. I'll give you her address.'

'Does she live with her parents?'

'Her father. And a housekeeper, a handyman gardener and a daily.' Adam scribbled an address and phone number on a piece of paper: York House, Elderton, Blackwood, Lancs. 'Elderton is a tiny village on the other side of Blackwood, and her dad owns most of it.' Tessa took the paper, remembering Sam Browne's warning. Sam thought that Adam was only interested in Lorna because of her father's money and power, but Tessa wasn't sure. It didn't fit in with her own opinion of Adam, whose honesty and integrity seemed essential to his appeal. Yet she had to admit she had not known him very long. Time would tell whether he had faults she had not yet discovered.

She turned to go. 'I'll let you know what she says.'

He smiled ruefully. 'She'll probably do that too. She'll be on the phone to me the minute you've seen her.' He sighed. 'I appear to be her only confidant at the moment. It's an honour I'd rather not have, but—well, I can't leave her in the lurch when she needs someone.'

'Quite.' Tessa could only admire his steadfastness. 'If you could persuade her that she ought to give up all these outside activities? I'm convinced she'd concentrate more on her work if she weren't always watching the clock, anxious to get surgery over.'

'I'll back you up, of course, but it may not be easy. She's spent all her life among the social set here. They ride, play golf and bridge, and she hates to be out of anything. But she must face up to the fact that her job is more demanding than anything the others do. Thanks for taking this on, Tess. She might just take it from you.'

'Well, I can only try.' Tessa opened the door. 'Good night.' She was already running up the stairs, before she realised that he was running up beside her. 'Adam,' she laughed, 'this is hardly necessary. I'm not going to be mugged or anything!'

'Just making sure. Foxleigh's a very rough neighbourhood.' He grinned. They stood looking at each other at her door. She knew what he was going to do; she knew she must hurry and get inside before he took her in his arms. But she stood quite still, and allowed it to happen.

He bent and touched her cheek with his, as though enjoying the feel of their faces together, smooth and warm. She smelt the strong manliness of him, the scent of the dark tendrils of hair curling over his ears. A sea of sensuousness began to overcome her, as he slowly, softly, moved his lips from her hair to her cheek, and from her cheek to her mouth, lightly, like the touch of a butterfly.

'G-good night, Adam.' She tried to speak steadily, as he kissed all around her mouth. She tried to push him away, but his embrace became firm, comforting, exciting—so right . . .

'Good night, Tess,' he whispered.

She found strength from somewhere, and backed away. His arms loosened reluctantly, and allowed her to go. Tessa made an effort to control her irregular breathing. 'Thank you for seeing me home—and remind me not to permit it in future.'

'I'll do that.' He did not move away. She turned round to open the door, very much aware of his strong presence, the firm, warm body only a fraction away from her. She couldn't help looking back over her shoulder as she stepped inside. Their eyes met, and the gaze lengthened. Each searched the other's face, with an unspoken longing, an inner communication, until Tessa felt tears rising suddenly at the back of her eyes.

'Oh, no!' she breathed, then she stepped inside quickly, and closed the door, before she betrayed herself and Guy's memory by kissing Adam Forrester with all the coiled, pent-up emotion he had engendered inside her that night.

She leaned against the door, the tears falling silently down her cheeks. She must leave this flat. It was terribly dangerous to live so close to such an attractive man. She knew she had almost given in to him tonight. Another time she might not have the will power—and that would be disastrous for them both. He would be disloyal to Lorna, who trusted and needed him, and she would be horribly unfaithful to the memory of the man she had imagined to be the love of her life.

She didn't know how long she stood there, but it was some minutes before she heard Adam's light footsteps going downstairs. He had been standing, as she was, full of the memory of the treasured moment of intimacy they had shared so briefly. She followed him—in her mind's eye. She heard him open his door, taking the coffee mugs through to the kitchen, walking slowly to his solitary bed . . .

'Guy, I haven't done anything wrong—' But as Tessa lay wide awake in bed, she recalled Sandy Singh's words—'Your London friends would not enjoy the life at Foxleigh?'

He was right. Even dear Guy would have mocked at her gentle affection for the baby rabbits, her feeling of sheer perfection at the glorious bursting trilling of the skylark. He would have trodden, unheeding, on the bunches of delicate snowdrops on Windmill Hill. He would have looked at the vivid plumage of the gorgeous pheasant only in terms of what a fine dinner it would make. He would have been bored here—where she was finding new pleasures every day.

Next morning, when she had done her rounds of the Rheumatology wards, she telephoned York House. The housekeeper it must have been who answered. No, Dr Goodison was not at home; she lunched at the Golf Club on Tuesdays. Tessa could have Dr Blake's number if it was important.

'I'll ring again. Do you know when she'll be back?' asked Tessa.

'I really have no idea.' The housekeeper was curt, and no wonder. She must have dealt with other unpleasant calls lately—from Jack Crowe, for a start. 'What name shall I say? She might call you back.'

Tessa gave her name, knowing very well that Lorna would be less than overjoyed to hear it, and was most unlikely to ring back. She rang off, sighing. The longer this interview was delayed, the more chance Lorna had of making more mistakes. She must try again.

But her telephone calls were not acknowledged that week. And Tessa was far too tied up with work to be able to make the trip to York House in person. She was frustrated in this. And she was also making efforts to avoid meeting Adam Forrester. She made it known that she was doing a paper on lupus—which was true. And she went up to her flat early each night, to read up on the latest work in all the relevant journals. Yet she knew that part of her was listening out for Adam's return each evening. She heard him come on Wednesday and Thursday. On Friday night she did not hear him come in at all, and this was confirmed by a careful examination of the car park. His BMW did not return, and unaccountably, this distressed her to the point of insomnia, though she would not admit it, even to herself.

On Saturday morning, she knew she would have to drive to Elderton to get hold of Lorna Goodison. Yet again her telephone call was put off. 'Dr Goodison had to go to Manchester on business with her father. If you'd care to leave your telephone number, I'll ask her to ring you . . .'

Tessa banged the receiver down. She didn't know if Lorna had given orders to avoid any phone calls, but probably she was just busy with her social life. It was annoying. She would have to go against Adam's wishes and telephone the woman at her surgery. At least she would be there in the mornings, and could not avoid speaking to her then. But the very fact that she was never available showed how difficult it would be for a patient to get her.

Tessa drove down to the Brown Cow for dinner in the evening. Annie's steak and kidney pie was plain but tasty, and it went well with half a pint of the local bitter. Sam Browne was kept busy, but he stopped as often as he could, to express his delight at seeing Tessa back at the inn. 'You're looking well, lass. The Foxleigh air is doing you good.'

'Thanks.' She knew she must be looking better, but it was probably nothing to do with the Foxleigh air. It was only that she had something to do—and so she no longer moped around, deep in her depression and sense of loss. She had come to life again; she knew it.

She ordered a second half pint and took it through to the snug, where she sat quietly in her usual corner, thinking how best to get hold of the elusive Lorna Goodison. Perhaps, after all, the only course would be to write to her and insist on a meeting. Yes, that was probably the only course left to her. Unless Adam could help.

Suddenly, as she was thinking of him, Adam himself slid athletically into the seat opposite to hers. 'Hello, Tess.'

'Hello.' She was glad to see him, but she must be careful not to let her feelings show. She must deal with him very impersonally.

'How did you get on?' he asked. 'What did Lorna say?'

She was suddenly prickly. He should know—he was the one who didn't come home on Friday night! 'I was going to ask you that,' she returned.

'I haven't seen her this week.'

Tessa looked at him carefully. He had never lied to her before. 'So you weren't with her on Friday, then?'

A rather joyful smile crossed his handsome face. 'Tess, my love, you do care! Now you've given yourself away. You've been keeping an eye on me. Now I know I'm not just the bloke that lives downstairs. Now I know that under that ice-maiden exterior you really care.' He reached his hand across the table and put it firmly over hers. 'You've just made me extremely happy.'

Tessa felt hot with embarrassment and she lowered her eyes. At that moment Sam Browne came over. 'That'll be Scotch, Mr Forrester?'

'Yes, please, Sam.'

The bluff innkeeper nodded, then he turned to Tessa. 'If you're free next Saturday, there's a good concert at the Free Trade Hall. I thought we could drive over, and look around Manchester, then have dinner. You did say you'd like to come?'

And because she had to wipe that look of triumph from Adam's face, Tessa made quite a show of being delighted. And she said yes with a lot more enthusiasm than she really felt.

CHAPTER SIX

THE city of Manchester proved to be a lot more fun than Tessa had expected. Sam had called for her in his modest little Ford early in the afternoon, and they had driven in along country lanes, that turned slowly into wide dual carriageways, and then into the great grey centre of the city itself. Unlike most men, Sam had proved patient and interested, as they wandered in warm sunshine round Piccadilly and Deansgate. He had even known where Miss Selfridge was, and knew what Benetton was, and Vidal Sassoon. Tessa was cheerfully tired when he suggested tea at Kendal Milnes.

'Well, we haven't done the Arndale Centre, but I guess we can leave that for another day.' They sat and drank tea, and Tessa slipped her shoes off under the table. 'You're a very understanding man, Sam,' she smiled. 'I haven't been window-shopping for ages—and you've been very patient with me.'

'Well, lass, there's not much use bringing you to see Manchester and then not letting you see it.'

She wondered what Sam's girl-friend had been like. But if Sam didn't want to talk about her, then Tessa wouldn't. She said, 'Well, I'm impressed. It's been fun. I can't remember the last time I did this.'

'Be with your last fellow, most likely?'

'Yes, my last fellow.' She found that it didn't hurt to say it. 'And he always got fed up after about half an hour. His attention would wander.'

Sam grinned. 'Well, I'd always go along with Beth.

Whatever she wanted to do was all right with me. Didn't do me much good, though, did it?' His smile faded.

Tessa asked with sympathy, 'Where is she now, Sam?'

'I heard from a mate of mine that she was back in England. That greasy tenor threw her out, he said, because she wanted to marry him.'

'Maybe she'll get in touch, then?'

'Nay, if I were too dreary for her then, I've not changed.

Tessa shook her head at him. 'You don't need to. But perhaps she has? Perhaps what she thought was dreary she can now see is sensible and trustworthy?'

He looked across the table, and there was gratitude in his eyes. 'Did you know you could make a chap feel ten feet tall?'

She smiled. She had not dressed showily today, but she had made more of an effort than usual. She wore a dark red fine wool dress with a swirling skirt, and a matching loose blazer. And as her feet now knew, she had dug out some smart shoes with a little heel. She had still not had her hair cut, but she had swept it up at one side with a slide, and it waved naturally on her shoulders. She saw from Sam's eyes that her appearance was appreciated.

The shop was emptying now; it was nearly closing time. Tessa reached for her shoes under the table. 'Where now?' she asked.

'I want to take you to a little bar I used to go to a lot, in Peter Street. I've booked dinner at the Midland. I know it's unimaginative of me—but I've always enjoyed it there. And it isn't far to the Hall from there.' Sam wiped the biscuit crumbs from his beard. 'Are your feet still killing you?'

Tessa laughed. 'I spend too much time walking round

wards to buy shoes that hurt! Come on, young man, I'll walk you off your feet, if you dare me!'

Sam found the little bar he remembered. It was called The Water Hole, and they went down a steep flight of stairs into a basement decorated with lurid jungle themes. There was little lighting, loud music, and plastic palm trees, oranges and lemons. Furry toy monkeys were placed in odd places. 'Well, what do you think?' he asked.

'It's so awful that it's lovely,' said Tessa with a grin.

'He does a very good cocktail here,' explained Sam. He held up a hand to the grizzled barman, who came out at once with two tall glasses on a plastic tray that looked like a banana leaf. 'Nice to see you, Vic. Tessa, meet old Vic, a friend of mine from the old days.'

The cocktails were good—refreshingly cool and fruity. 'My favourite—he calls it Safari Special. Don't worry, it's mostly tonic water and guava juice.' Sam was reassuring about the alcoholic content.

'Did you come here a lot?' asked Tessa.

'Beth did a course of singing lessons at the College of Music. I worked here for a while, so that I could be with her.' He smiled, and removed a tendril of plastic creeper from the back of his neck. 'That's why I began to think of a country pub—I got fed up with all the artificiality in town.'

'I know what you mean.' Tessa sipped her drink. 'Even I, townee that I am, feel the need for getting away from it sometimes. Now that I live in the country, I feel like a stranger in town.' And they turned to look at a group of students, with exaggerated hairstyles and black leather clothes. She smiled at Sam. 'But it is fun, isn't it? Just sometimes?' She watched the young people laughing and enjoying themselves, and she felt suddenly terribly old and wise—a whole lifetime wiser than they.

Dinner was simple but superb. Tessa chose a salmon salad, and Sam had chicken Kiev. They ordered a bottle of hock, and talked quietly in the elegant dining room of the Midland Hotel. It was easy to talk to Sam.

She mentioned the difference between the students and themselves, and he had the same feeling. She felt it was a good moment to get him to talk about himself, and he appeared glad to confide in someone. 'Dad was a miner,' he told her. 'He was chuffed when I got into university. I must have been a boring kid—never did anything wrong, worked like mad to see their faces when I took a good report home from school.' He was silent for a moment, then he said, 'They never liked Beth, said she'd never make me happy.' He looked down. 'But there again—they saw that I couldn't be happy without her either.' His voice trailed off, and Tessa recalled the time she had seen a tear on his cheek.

She said firmly, 'She's changed—she must have. I think if you met her again, you'd find she's grown up a lot.'

Sam beckoned the waiter to bring them coffee. 'I know where she's staying.' He looked at Tessa. 'But you can't know what it is to be so badly hurt that you think you'll never get over it. I'm frightened, Tessa, because I don't think I could take it a second time.'

She said, almost angrily, 'How couldn't I know? I've been through it too, Sam Browne. If anyone is scared of trying again it's me.'

'I'm sorry.' But she calmed down at once, recognising his need of calm and reassurance. He went on, 'Maybe we ought to encourage each other?'

Tessa was impressed with the solid majesty of the Free Trade Hall, and the streets they walked to reach it. It spoke to her of the prosperous days when cotton was King, and brought wealth and fame to this Northern province. And she liked the liveliness of the people in the streets, and the city brightness of neon signs, and the trendy restaurants and shops.

The concert was a lighthearted one, of Viennese music. It was calculated to send the audience home humming the tunes of the Strausses, after clapping and tapping their feet in time to the ever-popular melodies. Tessa and Sam walked down the wide staircase and out into a spring evening with hardly a breath of wind.

'It's been such a lovely day, Sam.' They were driving home along the country lanes, new-budding hedgerows shown up in the headlights. 'I've loved being in the city again. But you know, I'm really glad to be going back to Foxleigh.'

'It's been great for me too. Maybe we can do it again?'

Tessa nodded. But she felt a sudden guilty feeling, realising that this was her first date since Guy died. Perhaps she should have waited a year? She ought not to have enjoyed it so much. She ought not to have been able to push Guy to the back of her mind, and allow herself to have so much fun. She fell silent, the weight of guilt preying on her mind.

They stopped in the hospital car park, and Sam slid his arm along the back of her seat. Tessa sat forward, unwilling and suddenly unhappy.

'Don't I get a cup of coffee?' he smiled.

She felt mean then. 'Sure. Come on in.' She led the way upstairs, noticing the slit of light under Adam's door. She knew he must be in, the BMW was in its usual place. She wondered if he had noticed them draw up outside his window. It was so quiet at Foxleigh that every car that arrived was easily heard.

'Make yourself comfortable, Sam.' Tessa went to put the kettle on. 'Bathroom's through there. I won't be a moment.' She put cups, sugar and milk on a tray, and carried it through.

Sam was on the sofa. 'Dr Goodison was in the pub last night,' he told her. 'I guess she'd heard that Jack Crowe had gone back to Liverpool, and stopped his snooping for a bit.'

'Really? Alone?'

'No, with a man.' .

'Do you think the trouble has blown over, then?'

'No way. There's a date fixed for the inquiry. This is the lull before the storm.'

'Oh dear! So Jack Crowe has got all the stories he needs?'

Sam nodded. 'But he got none from me. I reckon it's better to see all and say nowt, as they say around here.'

Tessa nodded. 'And she was with a man?'

Sam looked scathing. 'Aye, her fancy man, Forrester. He'll stick around where there's money, believe me. I can tell when a man fancies a woman, and he isn't keen on our Lorna, that's a dead cert.'

Tessa was just handing him the cup and saucer. As he took it from her hand, she said coldly, 'Don't talk like that about Adam.'

'Tessa, I know. Why else would he hang around?'

She said, 'If you can't be civil about him, you'd better leave.'

Sam looked at her face, then he slowly put the coffee cup back on the tray. 'Maybe I'd better.'

She felt sorry then. 'No, Sam, just keep him out of the conversation.' She was appalled at the sadness in Sam's face.

He was standing up now, and he sighed. 'I was only

thinking of you. I've seen the way you look after him when he goes, and I don't want you to get hurt.'

'You weren't jealous, were you?'

He turned towards the door. 'Yes, I was as jealous as hell.' He spoke through gritted teeth. 'I could have knocked him down just as soon as serve him with his blasted whisky the other night!' And he strode to the door. He was out in a second, and slammed the door so hard that it bounced open again, and swung to and fro as Sam's footsteps tapped down the stairs and out of the building.

Tessa sat down, stunned and sorry. Everything had gone so well. Why did the evening have to end with such an explosion? She stared at the coffee, slowly going cold. Then she realised there was a draught, and got up automatically to close the front door.

There, standing in the doorway, wearing only a pair of jeans, as though he'd hurriedly pulled them on, stood Adam. His feet were bare and his hair tousled. He must have been in bed. 'Everything all right, love?' he queried.

She looked at him, surprised, and yet not surprised. They must have made quite a noise, with their arguments and Sam's exit. 'I'm sorry, Adam, we disturbed you,' she apologised.

'That's okay.' he was somehow inside the door now, and was closing it. He turned round, and their eyes met. 'I wanted an excuse to see you anyway. I've missed you, Tess. It's been a whole week since we talked—don't let it happen again.' And he pulled her gently into his arms, cradled her against his naked chest, the skin so warm and smelling of soap and man.

It was so completely comforting, standing there in Adam's embrace, hearing the beating of his heart. And

Tessa was weary—weary of her own loneliness, weary of struggling on, weary after a long week during which she knew she must have thought of Adam as often as he thought of her. She was weary of being brave, of facing the world alone. She put her arms round his body, feeling his tense muscles with caressing fingers. He bent his head towards her, and she meshed her fingers in his hair as he crushed her mouth with a hungry intensity, pulling him even closer towards her.

'Let me stay?' His voice was husky with longing, his lips soft and moist against her ear, her cheek, her neck. She yearned to agree. She needed him tonight; she wanted him as she had never wanted anyone else. But all the time they stood swaying together, wild thoughts of guilt fought in her head, fought to get out. How could she betray Guy—after only ten months? She had felt guilty about merely going to a concert with Sam Browne. How much more would she regret giving herself to Adam Forrester? A man who would soon be leaving for America, his lovely redheaded Lorna at his side?

'I can't,' she muttered.

'Why can't you?'

'Tell you tomorrow.'

'It's tomorrow now. Listen.' The cracked church clock was striking twelve. Adam held her as they listened, and his hands moved gently over her body, tracing the smooth outline from her chin downwards. She felt her breath catching.

'Midnight. You'd better go now, before I turn into a pumpkin.'

Adam drew back, his passion skilfully turned into affectionate laughter by her whispered words. 'You little witch!'

Tessa looked at him, knowing how much she loved

him at that moment. It hit her hard. She and Adam, they were so right together. They fulfilled each other's different needs, different facets of their personalities. They could talk as to no one else. They could work together, think together, love together—and their individual selves meshed, mingled and harmonised.

Her voice was suddenly small and quiet, like a child's. It was tiny, compared with the thunder of the realisation that she loved him. 'Adam—will you stay for a minute? Without touching me?' As always, he understood, he was on her wavelength. He nodded, seeing her need, and sat carelessly on the arm of a chair.

'You want to talk?'

She shook her head. 'I just want you to be near.'

'Bed is near.'

'It—it isn't enough.'

A new look came into the dark blue eyes as he studied her, then he stood up. His voice was curiously strangled as he said, 'I know.' Then he walked out, closing her door gently behind him. Tessa didn't hear his bare feet on the stairs, but she knew from the tugging at her heart that he was lying awake, his eyes wide open as hers were. He knew, and understood, the obstacles that loomed so high between them.

Tessa telephoned Gloria next morning, in a vain attempt to get back close to Guy. But Gloria had gone to some old friends who had an estate near Benidorm, and wouldn't be back till next month. Tessa felt that maybe she was not meant to get in touch. Maybe it didn't matter if she didn't contact Gloria again. Perhaps this was the first sign of the break?

At twelve, she saw Adam drive away in his BMW. Meeting Lorna, no doubt, at the Brown Cow. They would have their usual drink, then go on to one of the Country Clubs that Sam had told her about. She looked sadly at the spot where his car had been. It was no good: she was a fool to stay in this flat, so near to him, knowing that they were so strongly attracted to each other.

That was it. She would go for a drive herself, and she would go looking for house agents' signs of cottages for sale. Cheered by having something definite to do, Tessa ran downstairs and started her car. There was a warm gleam of sunshine breaking through the morning's clouds. Her mood was positive now, and she drove with the radio on, finding some equally optimistic music to accompany her.

She drove fairly haphazardly, so she was not surprised when she found herself at a familiar address—the market garden and farm shop run by Stan Ainsley, Joyce's husband. The shop was open, and Joyce herself was there behind the plain wooden counter, with a nice-looking young girl of twelve or thirteen. 'Hello there, Dr Tessa, nice to see you. I was just going to put the kettle on. Come along in.'

'Thanks, Joyce. Is this your daughter? She's like you.'

'Aye, this is Jennet, but happen a bit slimmer than me. This is Dr Daley, Jen.' The girl shook hands politely. 'Come away in, now. Jen'll mind the shop—that's how she earns her pocket money.'

'You might be able to help me,' said Tessa, comfortably seated on a chintz rocking chair in a sunny room in the seventeenth-century farmhouse. 'I'm looking for a place of my own.'

'That's nice. I've always thought those hospital flats were that gloomy, never a picture on the walls, or a change of curtains.'

'Yes. When I first came, changing curtains was the last

thing on my mind,' said Tessa, 'but suddenly—it must be spring, Joyce—I'd like somewhere that's my very own.'

'I'll keep my eyes open. Have you seen anything yet?'

'No, I'm just on a fact-finding trip now. I see the main agent round here is called Aspinwall.'

'Aye, that's right.' Joyce poured the freshly brewed tea. 'Young Tommy, he's taken over from his uncle, Josiah. I say "young" Tommy, but he's all of forty himself, with four kids of his own. He'll be the one to ring, come Monday.'

On their way to the gate, Tessa was introduced to Stan, a taciturn figure, hoeing his vegetable rows in the garden. 'There's a wee cottage on the Goodison estate, now, out Elderton way,' he told her. 'Do you know it? Happen you'll be driving round that side of Blackwood?' Stan's rich Lancashire brogue rolled from his lips like the rumble of thunder on the moors.

'Yes, I will. Thanks a lot.' Elderton way. Tessa knew she had some unfinished business out Elderton way. She would go to see the cottage. And then perhaps, if Lorna were in, she could manage to have that heart-to-heart, that had been successfully delayed by Lorna so far.

Elderton village was small but pretty, the houses clean and the gardens well maintained. But Tessa saw no 'For Sale' notice until she had passed through the village proper, and come to a field, shoulder-high with tall nettles, bluebells and budding pink campion. Almost hidden was a small thatched roof. Tessa got out of the car and approached it. Yes, there was a sign: this was the one. She smiled with delight. It was like a toy house, sunk down at the edge of the field, with little square windows and a path of crazy paving up to an old-fashioned wooden door with a brass knocker.

She was reminded of the childhood story of the ginger-bread house, that was charming and attractive, but owned by a wicked witch! But this was no witch's house. Tessa went inside the garden and walked all round it, peeping into the tiny kitchen, with its red-tiled floor and black coal range with an oven where she could imagine herself baking bread, and cooking Lancashire hotpot. She went back to the front garden. The name on the gate was faint, but she deciphered 'Silver Birch Cottage'. Yes, there was the silver birch, coming into fresh new leaf, in the corner of the garden. Tessa went up to it and touched the smooth grey-silver bark.

'What are you doing here?'

She looked towards the door. A tall, rather stout man with a florid complexion and a bushy white moustache was standing, shotgun under one arm, and a black labrador at his side.

'Good afternoon. My name is Dr Daley, and I'm interested in buying this house,' she told him.

The man's rather hectoring tone vanished. His watery blue eyes brightened, and he nodded affably and held out his hand. 'My name's Goodison—Daniel Goodison, and the cottage belongs to me. Would you like to look around properly?'

'Very much.'

'Where are you living now, Doctor?'

'Foxleigh Hospital.'

'Really, now, there's a coincidence. My daughter and I are due at a reception there next week—Sir Harold Oliver's.'

Tessa said how nice that was. 'I've met your daughter,' she told him. 'We were introduced by a mutual friend, Adam Forrester.'

The florid man had by now found the bunch of keys in

his coat pocket, and selected the correct one for Silver Birch Cottage. He nodded at Adam's name. 'Mm, I've known Forrester for quite a time. Used to be sweet on Lorna when they were younger. She ended it, though, and they've only got together again recently. Still the best of friends. I like him, always have. Clever chap.'

Tessa did not ask any personal questions; she didn't want it to be obvious that she was interested in gossip. They entered the little cottage together, Mr Goodison having to bend his head under the lintel. Tessa was just the right height. 'They must have been small people who built this,' she smiled.

'It suits you, though, Dr Daley. You're just the right size, made to measure, I'd say. Come on in.'

She was charmed with the entire place. It was dry, and in good repair. The only problem was the outside loo, and the absence of a bathroom. 'I like it, Mr Goodison. I'll contact your agent next week, and see about getting a surveyor.'

'Fine, fine. I must say I'm delighted to find someone small enough, and with such good taste.' He locked up carefully. 'Now, can I offer you a cup of tea? My house is only next door.'

'That's very kind, but I must get back.' Tessa shook hands with him. 'I'll see you at the reception, then.' She reversed the car in the narrow lane and made her way, still cheerful, back towards the main Blackwood road. She was pleased with the house, and Daniel Goodison seemed a decent enough man. She must find a builder, and get an estimate for turning the little lean-to at the back into a modern bathroom. It was good to have something positive to think about, instead of mooning over Adam Forrester.

Then she saw what must be York House. 'Next door',

Daniel Goodison had said. What he did not say was that it was a palatial Georgian mansion, with a pillared front porch, a tailored garden with a straight drive, and stables behind. So that was where Lorna lived. Definitely a pampered upbringing. Yet that was not generally known to interfere with a doctor's ability to care properly for her patients.

Tessa stopped the car and stood for a moment leaning on the metal railings. There were wrought iron gates, with the family crest picked out in scarlet, blue and gold. For a moment Tessa felt a twinge of genuine envy. Lorna Goodison had the lot—money, beauty, position, education, land—and Adam Forrester. Some people had all the luck! She thought of Sam Browne, bringing his school reports home to a miner's cottage to show his mam and dad. What a contrast! She knew which of the two she liked better as a person, too.

Then she heard the screech of brakes, as a car came along the narrow road far too fast, and thought she recognised the sound of that expensive engine. She stood to one side as the gleaming white Porsche roared round the bend far too quickly. The brakes screeched again, and the car came to a skidding halt only inches from her own car. Lorna Goodison pressed the button, and the electric window zoomed downwards.

She stuck out her fashion-model head. Beyond her, Adam Forrester could be seen in the passenger seat. Lorna's lovely face was ugly with anger. 'What the hell do you think you're doing, leaving your car there, right in my way!'

Tessa looked at her own car. It was not in anyone's way, but carefully parked close to the hedgerow. She saw Adam remonstrate with Lorna, and she looked at him for a moment. Then Lorna looked out of the car again. 'I don't care if it's the Queen of Sheba, she's still in my way! Would you mind moving your car? At once?'

CHAPTER SEVEN

TESSA surveyed the furious redhead, who gripped the wheel of the Porsche, white-knuckled. For a moment she could think of no reply to such manners, except silence. Adam moved first, opening the door and jumping athletically from the car. 'Are you all right, Tess?'

'Of course she's all right!' shouted Lorna. 'What about me? It's my car that nearly got scraped. Fancy leaving her heap just there!'

Tessa knew then what to say. She had to interrupt Lorna's flow of anger. 'Well, I have just been invited to tea by the owner of the house,' she said calmly.

Lorna's face went blank. If Tessa had not known all the trouble poor Lorna was going through, she would have laughed aloud. The other woman stared at her for a full minute before she spoke, and then her voice was harsh with bitterness. 'So you've got at Daddy too? I might have known! I could tell you were a sly one from the beginning!'

Adam opened his mouth to protest, but Tessa was quite close to the white Porsche. She said quietly, 'Lorna, you aren't doing yourself any favours, are you? I'm on your side—or didn't Adam tell you?' She saw Adam nod his head, but Lorna's fury did not lift, and Tessa took another step towards her. 'I think you're going to need me. Think it over.' And she turned on her heel. She got into her own car and drove off in the direction of Blackwood, without another look at either of them.

It was only when she got back to the flat that she started to tremble. She went to the kitchen and took out the half bottle of brandy that she kept for emergencies. This was an emergency. She poured herself a nip and sat down at the little kitchen table to think. She ought not to have driven off so quickly; it had been a marvellous opportunity to talk things over with Lorna. She ought to have been more patient.

On the other hand—maybe this little meeting would have made Lorna more receptive to common sense. She was certainly quick to fly off the handle; it must be that glorious red hair. Tessa sighed, suddenly picturing Adam—he would be comforting Lorna, in their beautiful drawing-room; she was sure the interior of York House was as imposing as the outside. And she felt a great twinge of jealousy, and tossed back the last of the burning brandy. What was the point of going over it all?

She went along to the doctors' lounge, where three or four juniors were slouched over the television. Sandip Singh was sitting in a quiet corner, reading a medical journal. Tessa went over towards him, and he looked up, smiling his big white smile. He was a perceptive person—and a kind one. She didn't want to tell him her troubles, but she did want to forget them for a while. She had just been called a 'sly one'. It wasn't a particularly bad thing to say—but she felt it was unjust, because it was not true.

She opened her mouth, ready to ask him if he thought she was more than average sly, but he spoke first. 'I'm glad to see you, Tessa. Which book do you recommend for the collagen diseases? I have read all the articles I can lay hands on, but I am confused. Is there a proper book that summarises all the latest work? Reading articles here and there is so scrappy—and some contradict each other.'

'You're right, of course. What are you reading now?' She looked at the article he had just put down. 'Oh yes, he's very good. He's Chief of a large department in Edinburgh. He's been working on lupus for years. And he's good on scleroderma too. He's very clear about treatment.'

Sandip shook his head. 'Fair enough. But what is the treatment? All I see is alleviation of the symptoms.' He threw down the magazine. 'Is there nothing that can be done for these people? You know, I never came across this problem in my country.'

'That doesn't surprise me. There must be many people with this type of auto-immune syndrome who never even know that they're ill. I guess in India doctors are too busy combating hunger, and the parasitic diseases, to have the time and money to pick up obscure problems that can only be diagnosed for sure in the laboratory.'

'Yes, you are right. It makes me think very hard, when I see all the heart transplants and the kidney machines in Britain, when more than half the world lacks primary health care. It frightens me.'

Tessa nodded. Without knowing it, Sandip Singh had effectively put her own tiny personal problem in its place with a bang. She was one of the privileged minority; she ought not to grumble about having an argument with Lorna Goodison! She smiled at Sandy. 'I wonder if you'll stay here, and get used to Western ways, or go back where you know you're needed?'

He waved his hands expressively. 'I want to be a surgeon, but after that, I make no predictions. What will be the use of learning how to replace these joints with

artificial ones, when there will be no one who can afford
to pay for them?'

'Surely that's not true?'

He grinned. 'Not only that, but Indian surgeons have
invented the Indian Hip, you know. Because the Indian
will squat on his haunches to chat, and the conventional
replacement joint would immediately dislocate. They
have adapted the socket so that this does not happen.'

'That puts me in my place!' Tessa had forgotten her
own problems now, and was thoroughly enjoying the
conversation. 'I was arrogant, Sandy—I'm sorry. It
would do me good to travel a bit, I suppose.'

A voice from behind Tessa's head said, 'Excuse me
—is this a private discussion, or can anyone join in?' It
was Adam Forrester. Sandy jumped up at once. 'Sorry
to butt in,' Adam added.

The houseman beamed. 'Come and sit down, sir. Let
me get you a coffee.'

Adam shook his head and sat down with a smile of
acknowledgement. 'No, thanks, Sandy. And less of
the "sir", if you don't mind. I've just dined with the
Goodisons, and hospital coffee would rather spoil the
taste of their fresh Blue Mountain, and the excellent
Benedictine he served with it.'

Sandy sat down, and waved his arms again. 'And you
come along and tell us poor people all about it? How
could you?'

Adam laughed. 'Well, it's Sir Harold's do next Saturday. You only have six days to wait for the feast of the
year.'

'Is it really as good as that?'

He nodded. 'It's superb. They get some catering
company from Manchester. Smoked salmon, sides of
beef—sorry, Sandip, I forgot you don't eat beef. There's

lamb too, and ham, and a trolley full of salad. And you can drink Benedictine by the gallon—but you have to wait six days.'

'Actually, I don't think I like it.' The young houseman left them after that, and Adam looked after him with appreciation.

'He's a good chap.' He turned to Tessa. 'Shall we make our way home too?' Tessa stood up. She could tell that he wanted to speak to her privately, and she was anxious to hear what Lorna had said. They started to walk along the corridor together.

'You've talked to Lorna, then?' she asked.

'Yes. Her old man didn't know anything about it —can you imagine? She hadn't told him a thing. No wonder she was edgy! I believe that underneath, she's feeling ashamed that she's let him down. You know, family honour, that sort of thing.'

Tessa looked up at the man by her side. 'She's a lucky woman,' she said quietly.

'Lucky?'

'I admire your loyalty. She's lucky to have you on her side.' Tessa tried to hide the jealousy that welled up in her. 'Did you ask her to cut down on her hobbies and other activities?'

'Yes. She didn't give a straight answer, but she must be thinking about it right now. You know she's coming to the reception?'

'Yes, Mr Goodison told me.'

'Mr Goodison? I thought you were joking when you said he'd invited you to tea. Do you really know him?'

Tessa nodded. By this time they had reached Adam's door. She hoped they could part tonight without any complications. 'I met him by accident.' She didn't say any more about Silver Birch Cottage; he would find out soon enough. And she wanted to avoid telling him why she was leaving Foxleigh; that would make it obvious how much Adam meant to her. 'He's quite a nice chap, I thought. Good night.'

'Wait. Don't you want to ask more questions about Lorna?'

She looked up at him with a little smile. Inside she was almost annoyed that he did not understand her feelings. 'I'll talk to her on Saturday.' The last thing she wanted was to hear Adam sticking up for Lorna. He was doing the right thing, but Tessa felt she couldn't hide her feelings for ever. 'Good night,' she said again.

'I—wait, Tess, I feel I must apologise for what she said to you.'

Tessa shook her head briskly. 'That's all right. I didn't take it to heart, you know—I'm not a silly teenager. Anyway, Adam, maybe she's right. Maybe I am a "sly one".'

He matched her smile with one of his own. 'You're a clever woman, Tess, very clever. I called you a witch, remember? Perhaps she was right. Don't you want to talk about it?'

If he had hoped to provoke a response from her, he failed this time. She shook her head and ran upstairs. This time she had her key ready. She opened the door and closed it again after her, before Adam had time to say or do anything more.

Tessa knew that she must find time during the coming week to be in on one of Sir Harold Oliver's operating sessions. She was looking forward to the reception, and she felt that watching him work would be only the polite thing to do. She had been at Foxleigh for several weeks now, and she ought to make time to attend at least one of his sessions, before meeting him socially.

She found herself with more than she bargained for, when she presented herself before a morning session in Theatre One. 'My houseman is delayed—An emergency admission,' Sir Harold told her. 'Would you mind assisting for the first couple of cases, Dr Daley?'

She had always been interested in orthopaedic surgery, but reading about it was vastly different from actually doing it. She hesitated. 'I'd like to, sir, but I'm a bit out of practice.'

'Not to worry.' Sir Harold was tall and slim, and his eyes seemed always looking into space, as though he was planning his next case. But they had a way of twinkling when you least expected it. 'You're the bright young thing who worked for my old friend MacFarlane at King's, aren't you? Go and get scrubbed up, Dr Daley. MacFarlane doesn't work with duffers.'

Tessa did so, feeling quite a tingle of anticipation. She was busy at the hot tap, making sure every millimetre of her hands was clean, and she failed to notice the man scrubbing up at the next basin, until Adam said quietly, 'You do look fetching in green, love,' and she turned, and felt her face turn scarlet, as he looked her up and down, obviously admiring her slim figure under the loose-fitting gown. He grinned. 'Come and assist me instead. I'll let Harry have Sandy for an assistant.'

Fortunately Mr Shepherd came up to Adam then, his gloves already on his hands, and his mask in place. Tessa said to Adam, 'Ask me again when you get back from the States.'

'Ah, yes, America. Do you know, Dr Daley, Foxleigh is looking more attractive than it has for years?' And he went smoothly past her to the adjoining theatre, where Sister was waiting with sterile mask and gloves. Tessa forced her eyes away from his tall figure and went through to Theatre One.

She was glad she had. Instead of a routine hip replacement, Sir Harold was operating on a woman of Tessa's age, who had been born with a hip deformity and had limped all her life. He was proposing to replace the joint with an artificial one which would eliminate the limp. He explained as he made the preliminary incisions, and Tessa was quick with clamps and retractors as needed, how they had made the measurements both from the existing hip, and from life-sized X-rays. He showed Tessa the prosthesis before he began to fix it in place, showing her how it had been modified to suit this particular patient.

She was engrossed. She was so interested, and so keen to make no clumsy mistake in front of the great man, that she almost forgot what Adam had said. Only when they had reached the point of putting in the final sutures, and the drainage tubes were carefully positioned along the incision, did she recall his words about Foxleigh. Had he changed his mind? Was it Lorna's doing? Or perhaps he was just making a joke of it all, to tease her. He had seemed serious enough about emigrating last time they had talked of it.

'Well done, Dr Daley. Pretty neat work for a rheumatologist!'

She jerked her thoughts back to the patient, who was being removed to Recovery. 'Thank you. It was interesting.'

'You're enjoying it here?'

'Very much. I didn't think it would be so rewarding.

'Then you'll stay on when Dr Bryn-Jones gets back?'

'I'd like to.'

'It might be an idea to put in for the Senior Registrar's

post.' Then Sir Harold was gone, but as Tessa removed her gown and cap, mask and boots, she knew he had paid her a great compliment. By inviting her to apply for a senior post he was, in effect, saying that there could well be a consultancy for her when the time was right. She left the Surgical Wing in quite a glow of optimism. Forget Adam Forrester and his ambitions. She was needed here, appreciated here. It was a good feeling.

Later, in her room, she found that the surveyor had written to her after his examination of Silver Birch Cottage. She smiled as she read it. 'Your dolls' house is in excellent nick. The thatch was renewed five years ago, and is good for another fifteen if you don't set fire to it. Proper report follows, but I'd say it's a good buy at the price, if you're five foot two or under. If not, extra insurance is advised against chronic headache or fractured skull.'

She wasted no time in rushing down to Joyce Ainsley's ward, to ask her who she recommended to make her a bathroom. Joyce, of course, knew just the man, and even offered to get in touch with him for her. Tessa returned to her hospital flat and looked around her in amazement, wondering why it had ever depressed her. She tidied it up happily, making plans in her mind for her little cottage. She went to the window and opened it wide before she went to bed. The evening was still slightly light, the air heavy with the scent of hawthorn blossom. She leaned her elbows on the sill, and drank in the peace and the stillness. How could she ever have thought it dull?

Then, in the echoing silence, came the clear sharp call of a cuckoo—those two derisive but resonant notes, from down by the conifers across the field. Disreputable bird that it was, its lucid song still had the effect of reminding her that it was really spring. It repeated its call, again and yet again, across misty fields and sleepy cottages. The stars were beginning to show now in the dark blue sky—the sky almost the colour of Adam's eyes . . . Tessa turned away suddenly. Those particular eyes were taboo from now on, eyes that were reserved for Lorna Goodison only to gaze into.

When Saturday morning came round, Tessa had almost forgotten that it was the date of the reception, so anxious was she to drive along to her own little cottage and go ahead with the plans she had already drawn up with the builder. Her own little house! She tried not to let it show, but she was hopelessly in love with it already, and full of ideas for decorating and painting.

She stopped off at Joyce Ainsley's house on her way to Elderton. 'I'm going to pick curtains for the cottage, Joyce,' she said. 'Will you be in Potter's as usual for lunch? It's handy for the market.'

'Of course—I'm a regular. Do you need any help in the cottage? Stan'll come along if there's anything that needs a bit of muscle.'

But Tessa wanted no help, needed none. It was all exciting and new, the challenge of making a home. In London she had never given it a thought. Clothes and perfume, outings and shows—that had been her life. She felt so much more satisfied with life now, as she went from stall to stall, comparing pretty flower prints, and matching scraps of material.

'Stan's getting all his vegetables in just now,' confided Joyce.

'Now? So I'm in time to grow my own potatoes? And beans? And lettuces?' Tessa had found yet another dimension to her happiness. 'Gosh, I might even find I have green fingers!' She smiled. 'I just hope the

directions on the packets are clear. And I'd better buy
a spade. This is fun, Joyce!'

Joyce Ainsley finished her soup. She said wryly,
'Well, Tessa, if you don't make it the first time, remember that Ainsley's farm shop stocks all you need.'

'Fair enough.' Tessa was anxious to get back to her
little house. The sun shone warmly; it might have been
June, not April. Tessa found a besom and swept out the
kitchen; it must be spotless when she moved in. When
her arms began to ache, she sat on an upturned tub at the
front door and enjoyed the sun's rays, as she leaned back
against the stone walls of her own little home.

She heard the shouting and giggling of a group of
village children passing by, but took no notice until she
heard some distinct words. 'There's someone in the
witch's house—look, sitting by the door!'

'It must be a witch. Another witch!' The voices were
excited, whispering but audible.

'Aye, it is. Look, she's still carrying her broomstick!'
And there were more hushed whispers as the children
crept past, looking back over their shoulders, enjoying
the sensation of being frightened.

Tessa watched them go, still holding the besom. She
recalled what she herself had said about witches—poor
old women who were blamed for things that went naturally wrong. She sighed deeply. Would she end up here,
old and crooked with arthritis? Perhaps. She had experi-
enced love twice in her life. One had died, a happy
memory of lights and laughter and fun. The other?
Tessa's mood saddened. The other was real, more real.
He was very much alive—and all his charm, his manliness, his beauty, belonged to someone else, a woman,
Tessa knew, who could never be good enough for him.
Such was the tragedy of life. She began to regret that she

had refused Adam her bed. Even that was perhaps better than having no memories of him at all . . . She sat idly crushing a lavender leaf from the fragrant new plant that sprouted by her own front gate, filling the afternoon air with sweetness.

She made her way back to Foxleigh, her mind lulled and peaceful. She would take over from Dr Finch when she got back. There would probably be nothing much to do, so she could shower at leisure, and get ready for the big reception. It would be fun.

Somewhere in the back of her mind was the thought that Guy would never have settled at Foxleigh. Their times together had been heavenly, but in Elderton, he would have been terribly bored, and their happy life together would soon have soured. Yet here she was, loving every bird's clear note, every yellow celandine and coltsfoot that decorated the hedgerows, every scent of new grass, new leaves. She lifted her hand from the steering wheel for a moment, the lingering fragrance of lavender—her own lavender—sweetening the air in the car as she drove.

'Dr Daley—Dr Daley, thank goodness! Dr Finch wants you in Ward Seven.' Tessa had just pulled up, and put the handbrake on. She switched off the engine.

'What is it, Staff Nurse?'

'An emergency, sent over from Blackwood Maternity —acute liver failure. They've just done an emergency Caesar, in case the mother doesn't make it—a premature Caesar.'

Tessa dashed at once to the ward. John Finch was in Sister's office, and Sister Jones was talking gravely to him. It was clear from their faces that the problem was serious. As Tessa hurriedly rinsed her hands, John explained. 'It was an ordinary pregnancy, but she went to the ante-natal clinic today, at thirty-three weeks. She's been a bit off her food, but never thought it worth making a fuss about. They checked her blood, and found severe liver failure, with no obvious cause. They took her in, of course, and she deteriorated so much that they operated to save the baby. The mother wasn't expected to live.'

'Is the baby well?' asked Tessa.

'Yes, in intensive care, but holding her own.'

'And we have to decide what's wrong with the mother?'

'Yes. Though it won't matter now, except as a statistic on her death certificate.' John Finch looked miserable. 'There's nothing we can do but nursing care.'

Tessa walked down the ward, to where the curtains were drawn round a bed. Sandip was standing beside it, where a blonde, almost unconscious woman lay, her skin golden with severe jaundice. Her notes said she was twenty-three. Poor soul! Tessa took her pulse. It was weak, and rapid. The woman turned to her and moaned without opening her eyes, 'My stomach!' Tessa put cool hands on the swollen abdomen, where the Caesarian wound was covered with a gauze pad. Yes, the liver was palpable beneath the ribcage.

'It's all right, Mrs Moore, I'll give you something to make you more comfortable.' At Tessa's words, the woman opened her eyes. The whites of her eyes also bore the telltale yellow of her disease. 'Is there anything you want?'

'My baby? Is she going to be all right?'

Tessa looked at Sandip, who nodded vehemently. She said, 'Yes, she's fine, and very beautiful. She'll have to stay in intensive care, because she's so young, but only for a day or so. What are you calling her?'

'Paula. We decided ages ago.' There was a slight relaxation in the tenseness of her face, then she looked up at Tessa, and the eyes became tragic. 'He'll manage, won't he? My husband? While I'm—while I'm here —until I—go home?'

Tessa said softly, 'There'll be lots of people to help. I'm sure he'll be fine. Now, I'd like you to rest until visiting time. You want to be awake when your husband comes, don't you?'

The woman gave a weak nod. Tessa patted the hot, thin hands, then returned to the office. 'You've taken blood, I suppose?' she asked.

Finch nodded. 'The lab is working on it now.'

'You suspect some connective tissue disease?'

'Well, it has to be a possibility, don't you think?'

'Oh, yes. She must have felt ill, but thought it was part of being pregnant. She never complained of anything until she was seen in clinic.'

Finch grumbled, 'Women come in two categories —the ones who never complain, and the ones who complain all the time. Poor lass, she's one of those who don't want to bother the doctor. And now—well, unless we're very lucky, there's going to be a motherless babe.' He shook his head. 'Why, oh, why?' It was a question he did not expect anyone to answer. He turned to Tessa. 'I say, you're late for the reception.' She noticed that under his white coat he was already dressed in his dinner suit. 'I'll wait for you.'

Tessa shook her head. 'No, don't bother, I'm on call anyway. I think I'll stay around the ward, John.'

'You can't do any more by being about fifty yards farther away. Come on, Tessa, you've been a physician for long enough to know that we can't do any more for her than is being done. Sister Jones is a capable woman, she'll call you if you're needed.'

'You're right, of course.' They walked slowly along the corridor together. 'But don't wait for me, John, I'd like to take my time. Somehow it doesn't seem to matter, when someone is dying . . .' She was appalled to find tears on her cheeks.

They stopped, as John Finch patted her shoulder. 'It's all right, I know how you feel. You can put a brave face on it most of the time, but unless you're a complete monster, it has to get to you sometimes.'

His few words, spoken in a calm and sensible voice, helped her to pull herself together. She had been through a lot since coming to Foxleigh. Falling in love had not been part of the plan, for one. Tessa took a deep breath. 'I'm fine now,' she said firmly.

'I'll wait.'

It was decent of him. Tessa appreciated his thoughtfulness. She took a very quick shower, then wound her hair up into a knot on top of her head. Now, her best earrings—the dangling diamonds, the only expensive jewellery she owned. She took out her long, deep blue chiffon dress. It was formal without being too revealing, with a round neck and long loose sleeves. As she twirled briefly in front of the mirror, she found herself thinking again that it was the colour of Adam's eyes . . . But Adam was not hers to think about. She forced herself to think calmly and rationally of Lorna Goodison and Adam Forrester as two acquaintances of hers who were to be married. When she saw them together, she was not—repeat not—to let it bother her a scrap.

She slipped on her strappy blue sandals, then looked at herself again critically. A touch of lipstick, and a squirt of Arpège in the general direction of her left ear—there, that would have to do.

She turned once more. Good heavens, woman, for once you look almost human! she told herself. Good old Sir Harold, for giving a party. And good old John Finch, for persuading her to go. Foxleigh was definitely a good place to be.

CHAPTER EIGHT

SIR Harold Oliver, as Tessa had already noticed in theatre, was a slim, superbly fit figure of a man. He gave the impression of taking regular exercise for his waist-line, of visiting a hairdresser regularly to keep his silver locks so sleek, and a manicurist to care for his long slim fingers. He looked very splendid tonight, and very much at home in a well cut dinner suit.

Lady Oliver was standing beside him in a very plain Crimplene gown of dark green, that looked home-made. But as Tessa was introduced, and had the chance of speaking to her, she saw that there was much more to Lady Oliver than was obvious at first glance. She was dumpy, of that there was no doubt, but she was cheerful, intelligent, and an excellent hostess. She was quick and tactful at spotting anyone standing alone. Introductions flowed elegantly and naturally from her tongue.

'I've been looking forward to meeting you, Dr Daley,' she smiled, and it sounded as though she really meant it. Tessa soon felt ashamed of her critical first opinion of this pleasant woman. Tessa had been influenced by Gloria Trethowan, whose own dress sense was perfect, but whose humanity towards those who put less stress on clothes was narrow-minded and petty. 'My husband tells me you stepped into the breech in theatre last Wednesday without a moment's hesitation.'

Tessa agreed. 'But I was apprehensive. Sir Harold seems to invent some new procedure each week. It was lucky that I was up-to-date with my reading.'

Lady Oliver showed her appreciation of this compliment with a jolly chuckle. 'Now, my dear, who shall I introduce you to? You must know several of these handsome doctors by now?'

'Please, don't worry.' Tessa saw that the queue to meet the Olivers had grown while she had been chatting. 'I'll mingle quite happily.'

'We must talk later.' And her hostess made sure that a waiter with a tray of sparkling wine was on hand before she turned away. Tessa refused a glass, and walked on into the hall. She felt very little like empty social chatter just now. She was still emotionally with little Mrs Moore, and felt she might snap if called upon to make conversation. John Finch had understood that, and left her to drift quietly into a corner on her own.

The Hall was not a very grand place, but it had been bravely decorated with flowers and potted plants. The red vinyl chairs from Outpatients were placed round small tables, and they were filling up quite fast. Tessa went across to the side door. It was curtained over, but she knew it must be open, as the curtain billowed gently, and she slipped through, almost unnoticed, to the paved path outside. The scent of the open grassy fields, and the pine forests that she saw every morning when she woke, was sweet and soothing, and she breathed in deeply, glad to get rid of the ever-present hospital smell of Halothane, disinfectant and last week's dinner.

She heard another step on the path, as someone else emerged from the Hall. 'Thank God, Tessa, I thought you'd decided not to come!'

Adam came closer. By moonlight she saw his handsome figure, the black dinner suit close-fitting, the white shirt catching the light. There was a red rosebud in his buttonhole. She caught her breath. She had never seen him look so stunning, so utterly irresistible. To hide the fact that she was overwhelmed, shattered by his magnetism, she tried to joke with him. 'I say, you look like an advert for after-shave, or chocolates!'

He came closer, smiling disarmingly. 'Well, at least it still fits.' He reached for her hand, drew her closer, and kissed her cheek softly, almost as a brother would. 'You don't look so bad yourself.' His face was very close to hers, as he looked over her face and hair with a very approving look.

She felt threatened, not so much by Adam, but by her own very disturbing emotions at his closeness. She said quickly, 'Where—where's Lorna?' She cleared her throat, and hoped he hadn't noticed her huskiness at his presence.

'She's up at the far end of the Hall with Daddy. I looked in, but I decided to wait for you. I've waited ages. Where have you been?'

'I was sent a patient from Blackwood with acute liver failure, and a weakly positive ANF.' She told him briefly about Mrs Moore. 'I'm waiting for more blood tests now. They may be different, now that she's had the baby.'

He nodded, understanding, as he always did. Tessa said, 'There was really no need to wait for me, you know.'

'That's your opinion.'

Slightly exasperated, she protested, 'But I'm not a child, Adam dear.'

'I know that, but it gives me a nice feeling to look after you.'

Tessa burst out laughing. 'Oh, that's rich! And here am I, thinking I was the one who looked after you. I cast myself in the role of your maiden aunt. After all, you do bring your troubles to me, don't you?'

In the ensuing mirth, he put his hand casually on her shoulder, so that imperceptibly they drew closer together. 'So we're both universal aunts, are we? Maybe we ought to set up in business together?'

She felt a shudder of pleasure at his touch, and she liked it too much to move away, as she knew she ought. Adam felt the response, and his grip tightened still further. Tessa was conscious of the stillness of the night, the warmth of the April air, the clear moonlight bathing everything in silver. She wanted to stay there for ever, but she knew she must take control of the situation, and soon. 'Adam, you'd better go and find Lorna,' she said. 'I promised to have a word with her. And they'll be calling me from the ward as soon as they get the results of Mrs Moore's blood tests.'

'Yes, sure.' His voice was reasonable, but his arm was still around her, and with his other hand he turned her face gently towards him. 'We'll go in, and we'll find Lorna . . . and we'll talk everything over, like sensible people . . .' and his lips were coming closer to hers, and his voice was like warm honey, his breathing irregular . . .

Tessa could hardly bring herself to move; her knees had turned to water, and she needed him to lean on, suddenly bathed in a cloud of surrender, yielding naturally to something powerful and beautiful and undeniable. 'Adam—no!' This must stop, and now. He was playing with her; she was just a recreation for him, when he was not with Lorna. This thought gave her sudden strength. He was not showing any sign of retreating, so she murmured provocatively against his cheek, 'My lipstick is on your collar.'

He started back. 'It's not!' Then he saw her expression

in the moonlight, and laughed in relief and frustration.
'You—you witch! You're manipulating me.'

She had escaped from his arms, and now she was able
to smile. 'I only wish I could. But you're your own man,
Adam, I can't fool you. You're the cat that walks by
itself—you go only where you want to walk.'

His voice was warm with affection and self-mockery.
'I admit it—I can't fool you either. And I won't ever try,
I promise.' Then he said, in a tone that caressed her with
a physical force, 'But I would like to kiss you.'

Tessa would like that too—all her natural instincts
said yes. But it was pointless. His Lorna was inside that
Hall, and he had no right to play like this, even though it
meant nothing to him. He meant no harm, but he was
doing harm innocently, not realising Tessa's vulner-
ability. She turned away suddenly, so that he could not
see her face.

Adam seemed to know it was time to stop. With a
gentle touch on her shoulder, he said, 'Right, Tess, let's
go. You're still lost in your memories, I think, still
thinking of your pilot. I'm sorry, I shouldn't have in-
truded like that.' His hand was firm and reliable on her
arm, as he led her into the Hall, where they both blinked
a bit at the light. She wanted to tell him that Guy was no
longer first in her thoughts, but she kept quiet. Let him
think it, if it kept him at arm's length.

Lorna Goodison's quick brown eyes saw them come in
together, and Tessa felt a blush touch her cheeks. How
much worse would she have felt if they really had kissed,
out there in the romantic moonlight. At least they could
face Lorna faithfully. It would do the poor girl no good
at all to think that her Adam was not totally on her
side.

She went up to her with a smile. 'I'm sorry I'm late,

Lorna, but I have a serious case in Ward Seven. Shall we talk now? I haven't much time.'

Lorna nodded. She looked ravishing, in a green and brown dress that picked out the highlights of her lovely auburn hair. It was swept back, golden and rich, like the feathers of the pheasants on Windmill Hill. But her face was worried, and she looked older suddenly. 'Shall we go over to that corner?' she suggested, and the two women went together and sat down where they could not be overheard. A waiter brought them a tray of wine glasses, and they each took one. Lorna set hers down without touching it. 'I've really messed things up, Tessa —I realise that now. It's been going on for too long, and I don't think there's any chance of saving things.'

Tessa looked at her, surprised. 'That's not true, Lorna. Don't you see? You've every chance.'

'What do you mean?' queried Lorna.

'I mean that admitting your mistakes means that you're on the road to not making the same mistakes again. If you'd denied it, then Jack Crowe's action against you would be justified. But now that you admit that you haven't examined your patients properly, then in future you'll treat them better, won't you?'

The other woman was very quiet, then she said softly, 'Are you really sure? I did examine Mother Crowe, you know. I wasn't negligent with her.'

'Exactly. And it's her case that's being examined, isn't it?'

Lorna nodded again, then she took a sip from her wine glass. 'But I know the others. You know—at least one.'

'I know about Harry Ramsbotham, and Sharon Billington. But they're not bringing any complaints.'

Lorna leaned back in her chair and sighed. 'I don't

know how it happened, really. I just seemed to have so many—other things to do. Didn't you find this a problem? That medicine would swallow your whole life if you let it?'

'I suppose I was lucky in that I worked away from home.' Tessa thought back. She had never been part of a 'social set' like Lorna. 'I did have a group of friends, but my fiancé was stationed at Lossiemouth, so I had little to do except work. Then I'd take my leave at the same time as he did, and we'd enjoy every moment.' She leaned forward and picked up her glass. 'Believe me, I do understand. Medicine is demanding. It involves sacrifices.'

But Lorna had seized on something else Tessa had said. 'Your fiancé? He's in the RAF?' And Tessa saw Lorna's face brighten. She realised that she had been a threat to Lorna over Adam.

To avoid speaking about Guy, Tessa said, 'Tell me, is there definitely going to be a court case?'

Lorna shook her head. 'I have to appear before the local Family Practitioner Committee. They're the first line. If they think there's a case to answer, then it may be taken to the General Council in London.' She looked down at her own pretty shoes. She reminded Tessa of Sam Browne's Irish setter, the brown eyes so wide yet so tragic.

Tessa told her, 'Well, after what you've said, I'll back you up.'

Lorna's voice strengthened. 'You'll testify for me?'

Tessa put out her hand, warding off the other's enthusiasm. 'No, wait—you can't let me be questioned. What about Harry Ramsbotham? They're bound to ask me what else I know. And Lorna, I won't lie.'

'And Sharon Billington.' Lorna's face darkened. 'You

know, I let that poor girl live on aspirins for a year, before I referred her.'

Tessa watched her, convinced now that Lorna was sorry for her previous neglect. Why else would she be so open and frank with her? If that were so, then she must already be improving her record, and giving all her patients their proper amount of attention.

Adam and Mr Goodison were moving across to join them, and Lorna stood up, to show that the private talks were over. Adam looked gratefully at Tessa, but said nothing. Mr Goodison said, 'Dr Daley, how do you do? It's very good of you to give your time like this. I hope I can count on you to appear at the hearing at the Town Hall?' He crossed towards Tessa, who stood up to receive his warm handshake. 'You don't know what a blow this has been to us.'

Tessa looked unhappy. 'I would rather—not say anything officially.'

'But you're a good witness, Doctor. With your reputation, the other members of the Family Practitioner Committee are bound to listen to you.'

'It isn't quite so straightforward.' Tessa tried to explain. She had a good name, and she had no intention of compromising it by being party to any cover-up of Lorna Goodison, however much she sympathised.

Daniel Goodison turned on his charm. He was a distinguished-looking man, and knew how to be charming. 'You couldn't let us down now? Not after admitting sympathy?'

Tessa shook her head, despairing. 'But don't you see? Sympathy isn't enough—specially against a clever lawyer.'

'Ah, but Dr Daley, the Chairman of the committee is a personal friend of mine. I play golf with the Administrator.' Tessa began to feel she was wasting her time. Both Lorna and her father had sailed through life knowing the right people. Only now did they have to realise that even friendship—in the end—cannot hide negligence.

'Mr Goodison—' Tessa hated to be so frank, but she knew that she was the only person who could say it, 'even friends in high places have their own reputation and integrity to consider. Look, I know that Lorna isn't doing what she did before. I'm confident that her patients will get a better deal now. But I can't lie for her.' Her voice was miserable. 'When is the hearing?'

Mr Goodison downed yet another whisky. 'The first of May.'

'Do you mind if I have a few days to think about it?'

He beamed. He thought he had her then. 'My dear Doctor, of course not. How about coming to dine with us next Saturday? We can have a final chat about it then, and I'm sure we can reach some satisfactory compromise.'

'Very well.' Tessa did not want to dine with them. For one thing, she would see Adam there—she assumed he was invited, as one of the family . . . It would be hard to see him there, and pretend that to her he was only a colleague, though to him, that was all they were.

She was relieved when Sir Harold and Lady Oliver descended upon their party then, doing their duty as hosts to circulate. Tongues loosened by champagne began to make more noise, and groups began to form and re-form, as people met old acquaintances, and took the opportunity of catching up on hospital gossip.

Tessa found herself talking to Adam, just the two of them. They were standing fairly close together when John Finch came over to join them. His wink was knowing—and annoying to Tessa, as he said, 'You two seem to be getting on very well. Of course, you're very close neighbours, aren't you?'

She was so angry at his insinuation that she said quickly, 'Not any more, John. I've got a place of my own now.'

She was secretly rather pleased at Adam's bewilderment. That would show him not to treat her like a plaything any more! John Finch smiled delightedly. 'Good—very good, Tessa. That means you're definitely staying on at Foxleigh. We must have made a good impression on you. When is the housewarming party?'

She said airily, 'I must have one, of course. But my place is so tiny I'll have to have you all in instalments.'

Adam, she saw, was longing to hear more, but trying to pretend that he knew already. 'You could have a barbecue, Tess,' he suggested. 'The weather seems to be holding beautifully.'

Tessa laughed. 'That's a possibility. But don't tie me down, or I shan't invite you!'

Adam seemed to forget John Finch at that point. His voice was cool enough for her to know she had got through to him. 'I wasn't thinking of tying you down, Tess.' She had shown him that she was not the pushover he had thought. He had probably decided that one more session in the moonlight would be enough to bowl her over for good. 'At least—not right now.'

The phrase upset her. Right now? Did that mean that he intended to try later? She looked up at the dark blue eyes, but this evening they gave nothing away. Suddenly Tessa's bleep startled them all. 'I must go.' She took the receiver from the wall set by the door. Yes, Ward Seven wanted her. She made profuse apologies to Lady Oliver.

'We must meet again, Dr Daley,' smiled her hostess.

'Thank you,' said Tessa. 'And thank you again for such a lovely evening.'

'Pop back if you can, won't you?'

She didn't bother to collect a white coat, but went straight to the ward. Sandip was in the office, holding the blood test results. 'There is nothing abnormal, Tessa, no anti-nuclear factor, nothing to suggest any connective tissue disease. What do you think?'

Tessa sat on the edge of the desk, reviewing the results. 'If I hadn't been told, I would say this liver trouble was caused by a virus. But John Finch said all the titres had been done, and nothing was found.'

'Then we are back to her pregnancy?'

'It's possible. If that's the case, then the fact that she had a Caesar ought to tell in her favour. We'll know in the next twenty-four hours, Sandy.'

'She's sleeping now. Shall I stay on the ward?'

'Certainly not.' Tessa ordered him out of the office. 'You've missed quite enough of the party already. Go along, Sandy, please. I want to stay—I really want to. I feel there might just be a turn for the better—and I want to be here when it happens.'

He nodded cheerfully. 'Only if you are staying on duty, you'd better change into something more comfortable!' And he went off with a wave.

Tessa had forgotten all about her clothes. She looked at herself in Sister Jones' small mirror on the wall. Of course, the upswept hair, the dangling diamonds, the delicate blue chiffon dress—all rather out of place here. She smiled. Ah well, it didn't interfere with her efficiency. She sat down at the desk and began re-reading Jane Moore's notes from Blackwood Maternity.

Night Sister Burns came bustling in. 'Oh, Dr Daley, I

didn't realise you were here. Do you want to see Mrs Moore?'

'Is she still asleep?'

'Yes, she's pretty comfortable now. She had something to eat. It's on her chart.' She scurried around Tessa, making her feel slightly in the way. 'Shall I ask Nurse Wright to make you a cup of coffee?'

'No, thanks, I'll go up to my room, Sister. But if there's any change, please let me know at once.' Tessa put the letters she had been reading back in the folder. The last letter was about the new baby, Mrs Moore's premature daughter. There was always the tiniest chance that by delivering the little mite early, they had relieved the liver failure. There would be no obvious signs of improvement tonight, so Tessa might as well get some sleep.

But she stayed for a little while longer, chatting to Sister Burns, who seemed quite glad to have company. The ward was hushed, the lights on minimum. Nurse Wright sat demurely in the middle of the ward, reading a paperback by the light of a small hooded lamp. It was very late when Tessa slowly made her way back to her flat. She let herself in very quietly. There was no sound in the flat below, and no light.

Tiptoeing, she removed her dress and hung it up. Then she jumped, at a knock on her front door. Perhaps it was the ward? She put on her housecoat and tied the belt firmly round her waist, then went to the door.

Adam Forrester smiled. 'I couldn't sleep,' he announced.

Tessa looked scathingly at his dinner suit. 'Forgive me, but you don't seem to have tried very hard.'

He put his head slightly on one side. 'Nightcap?'

'I'm on call.'

'Tess?' there it was, the liquid honey. He knew how to use it.

She opened the door wider and he walked inside and straight to the kitchen, clicking on the light and taking the kettle over to the sink. She watched as he made instant coffee, taking the cups deftly from the cupboard and the spoons from the drawer, as though he lived there himself. She allowed her thoughts to wander, imagining what it would be like to be married to him, to know that he would always be around, always . . . He said quietly, without looking at her, 'What are you thinking?'

'Just how dreadful it would be to live with somebody else. They'd always put things away in the wrong drawers.'

He looked up for a moment, with a little smile. 'If that's the only problem, I think we could soon come to terms with that.' 'We?' Tessa looked away as he poured the coffee. 'Go and sit down.'

She obeyed, taking the chair, and not the sofa, to discourage him from becoming more friendly than she wanted. He carried the tray in. Tessa felt a lump in her throat, as she saw two cups of coffee on the tray—and a tiny glass jug containing the red rosebud from his buttonhole.

He smiled. 'There, that's just to say thank you for what you did tonight.' For a moment they faced each other, their eyes wondering just what the other was thinking, then Tessa relaxed into a smile. Adam smiled back, and loosened his tie. They were at home together, in spite of all the tensions and problems that surrounded them both. 'That's better.' He handed her the coffee.

'Thank you.' She had stopped pretending. He knew she was fond of him; he would know if she tried to pretend otherwise.

'Tess?' he queried.

'What?'

'Where are you going to live?'

'Does it matter?' she shrugged.

He nodded, and the loosened tie and the unruly hair made him look boyish and a little vulnerable. 'Yes, very much. I don't like changing neighbours—it's unsettling.'

'In case you want to borrow a cup of sugar?'

'Yes.'

'I'm sure the next person to live here will lend you some,' Tessa smiled.

'But the next person to live here won't be you.' He spoke in a very low voice, and made the simple statement of fact sound like a grand tragedy.

'That's right, Adam.' Her voice was light, although she was touched by his sincerity.

'I thought you—would have told me you were thinking of moving.'

'I would, of course, but things moved so quickly, and you weren't around when I first saw the cottage. Then, of course, I was busy finding builders to put in a bathroom, and choosing curtains, and all that domestic stuff. You would have been bored stiff.'

He stood up suddenly, and the look on his face was real and raw. He saw her look and turned away to stare out of the window. 'God, Tess!' His voice was a hoarse whisper. 'You don't care. You really don't care, do you?' And to her horror, he covered his face with his hands and went very quiet.

CHAPTER NINE

TESSA was tongue-tied, as she stood up. Adam still stood motionless by the window, and she felt she ought to go to him. He took a deep breath and took his hands away from his face, but he still stood looking out over the moonlit fields. She felt an almost physical need to go to him, yet it would be pointless. He ought not to be here, when he was committed to Lorna Goodison. He ought not to be upsetting Tessa's peace of mind—especially as she had a job to do, and could not afford to be bothered with Adam's problems when she was on call, and must stay cool and collected.

It was difficult, but Tessa did it. She turned, sat down again, and began to drink her coffee, as though she had noticed nothing unusual. Only the slight rattle of the cup on the saucer showed that her coolness and self-control was only superficial. She said quietly, 'Your coffee's going cold.'

'Hmm.' Adam turned, and she was relieved to see that he had regained a certain amount of twinkle in his eyes. 'Right, Auntie.' But they exchanged a long look, which Tessa tried not to interpret, before he came back to his chair. He drank the coffee at one gulp, sitting on the arm of the chair. 'I'll let you get some sleep. I'm sorry, Tess, it was selfish of me to come and interrupt you so late. Bless you, you're too sweet to tick me off when I deserve it.'

She watched him walk to the door, then something snapped, and she began, 'Adam—'

He stopped, not turning round. 'Yes?'

'I'm off duty tomorrow afternoon. I'm going to the cottage to measure up for carpets, if you'd like to see it. If you're around, of course.'

His voice sounded suspiciously pleased. 'It's a date.' He didn't turn, but there was something in the set of his elegant shoulders that radiated satisfaction. She watched him go, glad that he had not turned round and seen the naked adoration in her eyes. And she tried to pretend that she had invited him only as a friend and colleague—as she would have invited anyone who had expressed an interest in her cottage.

There was no official ward round on a Sunday, but when Tessa was on duty, she liked to keep herself well informed about the patients. Some of her rheumatology patients were on the latest drugs, and although she did trust the nurses, she liked to ask questions herself about side-effects. Occasionally she envied the surgeons— once they had done the cutting, the rest was nursing and physiotherapy, but with Tessa's patients, they required constant and stringent supervision, until she had found the correct therapy that suited the individual. But on the other hand, it made her job more interesting, because she got to know her patients so much better.

Mrs Moore was stable—no worse, but no better. If she could hold her own for another day or two, there might be grounds for hope. Tessa congratulated her on looking so well—though the jaundice had not faded yet. 'At least your blood tests were normal from our point of view. If you'd prefer to be transferred back to Black-wood, it can be arranged.'

But Mrs Moore had not wanted to. 'It's nearer for my husband to come here.' Her voice was very weak;

it was not easy to be optimistic.

Joyce Ainsley wasn't on duty that weekend. Tessa paid a brief visit to little Lizzie Stott, her patient on a trolley. Joyce's ward, as usual, was more relaxed. There were no serious cases, only poor chronic arthritics, who had developed philosophical and amusing attitudes to their plight. Tessa never heard any of them complain.

This morning, Lizzie had pushed her tea trolley up by the bed of a new patient, a stout and rather coarse old woman, who smoked whenever Sister turned her back, and had a fund of funny—and rather rude—stories. Tessa stood for a moment, watching the group that had gathered round her bed. Sister whispered, 'She passes the time for them, Dr Daley. It's better than having a moaner in the ward.'

Tessa smiled, 'Much better.' And she studied the charts of the patients, while the old woman held forth in a rich Liverpool accent.

'And there was this porter—nice lad he was and all, he'd put us in our wheelchairs, and nipped us over the road to the Queen's Arms. That was when Sister wasn't around, and we wuz supposed to be in day-room, like.'

'This was in Liverpool, Jessie?'

'Aye, city centre, luv, right across road from hospital. I tell you, it were better medicine than the muck the doctors give us. A couple of pints of ale, then he'd tek us back—some of us fast asleep. Well, there was one day when he took us over, and had to go home because his wife was took ill, so he left us in the pub. The landlord closed up at three, and didn't come back till five-thirty, and the porter didn't come back for us till seven. Ee, it were a laugh!'

'Did you get into trouble?'

'Porter did—he were fired. But worse than that, he'd

made me miss putting a bet on a horse in the three-thirty at Haydock, and it come in eleven to one. Aye, I gave 'im a flea in 'is ear that time!'

There were many admiring murmurs at this story of life in the big city. Tessa gave a sidelong smile at Sister. 'You must find your education is broadened quite a lot?' she remarked.

Sister nodded. 'As Sister Ainsley says, Ward Five is the entertainment centre of the North. At least we never get bored!'

In a considerably lighthearted frame of mind, Tessa came off duty and went round to the car park. She was wearing light cream slacks and sweater of a casual elegance she had bought in Knightsbridge the previous spring. She saw Adam's BMW in the car-park, but of Adam there was no sign. Ah, well—her invitation had been very casual. Perhaps he was busy. She was rather relieved that he had not shown up; last night had been rather too intense for her comfort. She looked across at the old twisted oak tree, noticing with pleasure the tiny leaf buds were bursting at last, almost the last of all the trees around the hospital. It was lovely to see the gnarled old branches proudly showing off their tender new green.

She flung her jacket into the back seat. By now the sky was almost cloudless, the sun warm, and the birds noisy in their appreciation of the fact. Tessa started her engine fairly loudly. If Adam had been in, he would have heard it, but there was no sign from his window. She smiled to herself. Yes, he probably realised that their flirting had been a bit over the top last night. She thought again of his choked voice, the way he had suddenly turned away, the words that burst from him, as though against his will . . . She realised that she was sitting gazing into space, and jammed her foot on the accelerator, annoyed at herself for a moment. She was surely not daft enough to hanker after a man who belonged to someone else! Yet they were so comfortable together, such very good friends . . .

She drove down to the Brown Cow. A glass of ale and a chat with Sam would be pleasant before she went over to Elderton. But she hesitated when she reached the inn and saw a certain white Porsche standing outside under the new leaves of the honeysuckle that climbed up the front wall. Then she took a deep breath. Why let Lorna's presence stop her doing what she had come to do? She walked into the bar and sat on a stool at the counter.

Sam beamed, 'Tessa love, it's been a long time.' His words were quietly welcoming, as he drew her a half-pint without being asked.

'Well, I didn't intend it to be,' she explained, 'but you know doctors—they're very unreliable people. Their patients always come first. Try breaking a finger, then you'd see how much attention you'd get!'

He laughed through his piratical black beard. 'Ah, knowing my luck I'd get put in a ward with a dragon of a Sister, and a consultant who came to see me every six weeks.'

She smiled, and raised her glass. 'Cheers, Sam. Here's to my new house.'

'You're moving?' he queried.

'Not far. I've bought a cottage in Elderton.'

Sam reached down and picked up a dark green bottle. 'Then this is on the house.' He poured two tots of brandy. 'A long and happy residence in Elderton.' They both drank. 'I'm that pleased, Tessa. I didn't think you'd stay around here, somehow. I'm glad to like us that much.'

'Why shouldn't I like it?'

'You with your fancy London background and all.' He shook his head. 'Well, well—Elderton, eh?'

Just then there was a whiff of an expensive perfume, and Tessa turned to see Lorna Goodison at the bar. She managed to speak naturally. 'Hello, Lorna.'

Lorna gave her a vivid smile. 'What can I get you, Tessa?' She opened her purse, her fingers tipped with scarlet nail varnish. But it was not the nails that Tessa noticed, but the diamond solitaire on the third finger of her left hand, shooting daggers of blue-green light from its expensive heart. 'A large gin and a large Scotch, Sam, please. And you, Tessa?'

Tessa gave a cardboard imitation of a smile. 'I'd better stick to brandy, please.' She felt she needed another, after the sudden attack on her feelings by that giant of a gem.

Lorna picked up the drinks she had ordered. 'See you next Saturday, Tessa?'

Tessa picked up the glass Sam had set before her. 'I'm looking forward to it,' she lied, and sipped her drink. She couldn't for the life of her look round at Adam now. To think he had been so tender and sincere last night —the eve of his own official engagement! She knew she had no claim on him, but she cared—and it hurt badly to be pierced to the heart by that chunk of blue ice on Lorna's finger.

Sam leaned over and whispered, 'Tessa, you'd better not drive with that little lot inside you.'

Tessa nodded. 'Will you drive me, please? Can you get the rest of the day off?'

'Is it my birthday?' he grinned. 'Annie'll pop down and take over. She's offered many a time, but I've never asked her before.'

Tessa took another sip. 'Then ask her, Sam. Let's go and eat somewhere nice, then I'll take you to see my little grey home in the west.'

'That'll be great. I'll be a couple of ticks.' He turned to the telephone at the back of the bar. Little Annie Blunt came bustling down at once. Tessa finished her drink, and linked her arm firmly into Sam's as they walked out together. She didn't look back, but somehow she knew that Adam would be watching, and she gave Sam an especially warm smile.

He took the wheel of her car. 'I'd like to take you to a little place up on the moor. Ever been up there?' He pointed in the direction of Windmill Hill.

'I've never been out to eat, except your place and Potter's Bar.'

'Then I'll take you to the Belfry. You'll like it.'

'Why?' she queried.

'Because it's cute and small and genuine, and the food is excellent.' He was soon off the main road, taking a little winding lane that lead upwards to the top of a moor. The Belfry was a converted row of cottages, with a thatched roof and painted black and white. There was a lot of wrought iron outside. Inside was the original slate floor, and a few tables with damask cloths. The clientele was small, but clearly consisted of people who knew it was worth the trouble to tackle that narrow winding lane. Sam led the way to a table by the window. 'Now, Tessa, what do you think of that?'

'Lovely.' She sat down happily. Outside was a green meadow, dotted with daisies and buttercups, sloping down to a duckpond, on which floated four ducks, posing as though for a postcard. Tied to a post was a white goat. There was a wooden sign nailed to the post, advertising ducks' eggs and goat's milk.

It was perfect; the old house emanated peace and contentment. They ate fresh salmon, with new asparagus in a white sauce with a touch of garlic. Everything was superbly served, and Tessa savoured every mouthful. 'How did you find this place, Sam?' she asked him.

'Word of mouth. In my job, I get to hear all the latest news. You hear all sorts behind a bar that you're not supposed to hear.'

'Like some of the untrue stories about Lorna Goodison?'

He countered her question with one of his own. 'I never reckoned you thought much of that woman, Tessa. You aren't trying to stick up for her now, are you?'

'Not specially. Just for the truth.'

Sam finished his salmon and put down his knife and fork. 'Well, you're a right one, and no mistake. I reckon I'm not a bad sort of chap, but I wouldn't stick my neck out for the likes of Lorna Goodison, and that's a fact. She'd do me no favours, that's for sure.'

'Don't you see, Sam? That's why we must. We have to rise above any pettiness, and stand up for what's right.'

Sam drained his glass of lager, then nodded slowly. 'Aye, maybe you're right. But we're not all saints, Tessa—not by a long way, we aren't.'

'Neither am I. But I'm thinking that if I were in a court of law, and facing a lawyer, after swearing to tell the whole truth—you see my point? We can only repeat what we honestly know to be true.'

'So help me God.' Sam signalled for coffee. 'When you look at it like that, I reckon all I've heard is just that—hearsay. I couldn't swear to any of it.'

'Yet you've judged her, haven't you? You've decided she's a baddy?'

Sam shook his head, grinning into his beard. 'Tessa Daley, you should have been a lawyer yourself, woman! I can't keep up with your arguments.'

She smiled. 'Finish your coffee, Sam. I want to see Silver Birch Cottage now that the builder has finished.'

'I've finished.' He set down his cup. 'Billy Blackshaw's been at it again, you know. Now that you mention the name, there was talk of it being sold, and Billy overheard, and said, "Someone has bought the witch's cottage in the bluebells." Is that the one?'

'Yes, that's the one. And it's beautiful.' They walked out, stopping to stroke the silky head of the mild-eyed goat. 'It was knee-high in bluebells when I first saw it—like a fairy tale. I've cleared some of them now, and I'm going to plant vegetables.'

'Well, Billy's away with the fairies anyway. I think this talk of witches gives him the only bit of excitement in his life.'

'It doesn't bother me.' Tessa took the wheel, and as soon as they had negotiated the steep lane, set off at a good rate towards Elderton. She pretended not to be interested as they passed the wrought iron gates of York House, but through the corner of her eye, she saw that the Porsche was drawn up at the grand doorway, and she tried to blot out the picture of the three of them celebrating the engagement, toasting the happy couple in champagne . . .

'Well, Sam, this is it. What do you think?'

He got out of the car. 'Silver Birch Cottage.' He looked at the sloping thatch, cosily covering the small mullioned windows, and nodded in approval. 'Well now, I never even knew this was here. What a find! You'll be looking forward to moving in.'

'I can't wait,' she smiled. 'I'm seeing the carpet people

on Wednesday. Will you give me a hand with a few measurements?'

'Surely.' Tessa showed him round, glad to have his appreciation. When they had made a note of the floor measurements, they sat for a while at the door in the spring sunshine. A clumsy bumblebee blundered among the remaining bluebells, and an ecstatic thrush carolled to the world that he had found the ideal nesting place in Tessa's back hawthorn hedge. There was a wooden bench under the front window. Tessa said happily, 'I'll make a tiny lawn here, and plant pink roses all around it. And see, Sam—my own lavender bush!' She laughed at herself. 'Oh, whoever thought I'd enjoy being domesticated so much? But it is such fun.'

'I can see what a nice thing it will be to come home to such a cute little place after a hard day at the hospital.' Sam leaned back against the warm stone of the cottage wall, and Tessa could see that he already saw himself as a regular caller.

'I'm sorry I can't offer you a cup of tea,' she apologised. 'The water is on, but I haven't bought anything for the kitchen yet.'

Sam roused himself. 'Ah, I've seen to that.' He went to the car and took out a bag he had put in the back. He set it down, then brought out two glasses and a half bottle of champagne. 'There. Now we can drink to the latest resident of Elderton. God bless her, and all who sail in her!'

'That's so sweet of you.' She watched Sam ease off the cork, which made a most satisfactory pop. Laughing in the sunshine, Tessa threw back her head, holding the glass high, so that the bubbles from the champagne fell on her face. Sam leaned over, and clinked his glass against hers, then he kissed her on the cheek. It was then that Tessa realised that a white car had just driven slowly past the front gate. It was too late to see who was in it.

It had been a lovely day, but when Tessa got back to Foxleigh her first thoughts were of Mrs Moore, and she rang the ward. 'Still the same, Doctor. It might be my imagination, but the eyes might be a bit less yellow.'

'I'll come down.' Tessa felt a tiny jump of hope. She never wanted to lose a patient, even one who was old, and this young mother was a life she wanted more than anything to save if she could.

'Hello, Mrs Moore—may I call you Amy?'

The woman nodded weakly. 'Yes, of course. It's a silly name. I was called after an old aunt.'

'It's very pretty. Now, let's just have another look at your tummy. Sister thinks the jaundice is slightly better.'

The woman lay back, her fair hair in damp streaks across her forehead, while Tessa examined the skin over her chest and abdomen, and felt gently for the edge of the enlarged liver. The Caesarian wound was clean and healthy. Tessa pulled down the nightdress again. 'Good, Amy. And I see from your chart that you've eaten today.' Soup, bread and half a banana—that was encouraging. The poor lady was not yet out of danger, but there was still a tiny chance. Tessa patted her hand. 'I'll see you again before you settle down for the night.'

'Thank you, Doctor. You make me feel better when you look so pleased with me.' Tessa kept up the smile until she moved away. Amy Moore didn't know how hard it was to keep up that smile, when hope was so slim.

She hadn't bothered about a white coat, and was still wearing the cream slacks and sweater she had been out in. After a few words with Sister, Tessa wandered along the corridor towards the doctors' lounge. Sam had begged her to come back to the Brown Cow with him, but she had made an excuse. She didn't want Sam to get too fond of her.

But she had only walked a step or two away from the ward when she saw a tall figure standing as though waiting for her. She knew, by the width of his athletic shoulders and the darkness of the curling hair, that it was Adam Forrester, and her heart lurched ridiculously. Why did she respond to this man so physically, when he was buying diamonds the size of golf balls for Lorna Goodison? Surely her common sense ought to control her heart.

He fell into step beside her. 'How's your patient?' he enquired.

'Holding her own, thank God.'

They walked in silence. Then he said, 'I saw you this afternoon. That's your cottage, is it?'

'Yes.' It sounded a bit curt, so she added, 'I'm getting my carpets in on Wednesday.'

Again a silence. They reached the outer door and crossed together the stretch of path leading to the doctors' flats. Adam opened the outer door for her. 'Have you eaten, Tess?'

'No. We had a big lunch. Have you ever been to the Belfry?'

'I've been.' His voice was toneless.

They climbed the stairs to his door, and she said, 'Goodbye.'

'Wait. Have a drink?'

She wanted to, but the sight of that diamond rankled inside her, and she felt her emotions beginning to wind up. 'No, thanks.'

'You sound tense. Come in, please, Tess. There's something I'd like to say to you.'

Although she knew he could have nothing to say that she wanted to hear, Tessa obeyed her heart rather than her head, and went in as he stood aside holding the door open. She walked through to the sitting room and sat down on the edge of a chair. Adam went to the kitchen. 'Coffee or whisky?'

'Coffee, please. You make nice coffee. And I've had enough alcohol for one day.'

'I saw you.' A rather reproving tone, she thought.

'You did?' She pretended she had not seen the Porsche go by.

'You know, you really ought to be careful of gossip. If you must carouse, do it inside, where people can't see you.'

Furious, she snapped, 'Adam, who the hell do you think you're talking to?'

'I'm only thinking of you. You have a good name around here, it would be very easy to lose it.'

'Like Lorna lost hers, you mean. It's none of your damned business!'

'That's a childish thing to say,' he said coldly.

'It's true, though, isn't it?' Their voices were getting higher, their comments sharper and more acrimonious. 'I thought you'd asked me in for coffee, not for a penny lecture that has nothing at all to do with you!'

He turned on his heel and went into the kitchen. Half of her wanted to go and hug him, the other half felt a great anger. He had allowed her to fall so deeply in love; he even spoke to her as though he had some sort of right over her—yet there he was, engaged to another woman. The cheek of the man was beyond belief!

Usually, when they had started to argue, they had dissolved into laughter after a very few minutes, part of their being cosy and natural together. Tonight was different. Adam did not stick his head around the door while he was making the coffee. He did not make some joking remark as he usually did, gently teasing the anger out of her, so that they always ended up as friends. Naturally enough. He must be realising that he had no rights over her, and ought not to have invited her into his room.

Something made Tessa think of a child she had once seen, who was furiously jealous of his brother's new toy. His expression had been exactly like Adam's, as he came into the room and put down two cups of coffee. It made her able to smile. She broke the prickly silence with a gentle voice. 'Adam?'

He looked at her, his face hard and cold. 'Yes?'

'Are you jealous because I took Sam Browne to the cottage first?'

'What rot! I couldn't care less.'

Tessa looked down. Of course, she had been foolish to think it. What did he want with Silver Birch Cottage, when he would shortly have the whole of York House to play with? She swallowed a lump in her throat, then she stood up, ignoring the coffee, and left his flat. She ran upstairs fast, managing to get inside and close the door before her tears actually spilled over.

On her little table, where he had left it, was the tiny glass jug with the red rosebud from his buttonhole. Trying to control her sobs, Tessa took the flower and screwed it up in her hand. Then she ran to the window and threw it down to the car park. It was childish—but it relieved her feelings.

CHAPTER TEN

THE following week glowed with the most perfect April weather ever recorded. The sky was virtually cloudless. The trees at the bottom of the field exploded into full leaf. Patients were allowed to walk around the grounds, to practice walking with their crutches and their metal supports, their smiles showing how much better they felt in the warm, comfortable spring.

Tessa had felt a lightness of heart too. Perhaps with the last desperate act of flinging that rosebud from her window, she had exorcised the influence Adam Forrester had over her. She went through her wardrobe, digging out cottons and silks she had not worn for months. She sent her winter clothes to the cleaners—in April. Sister Ainsley had warned her, with true Northern caution, 'Never cast a clout till May be out.'

'But Joyce, look—it's already in bud.' And indeed, the hawthorn hedgerows were producing buds of may blossom at least three weeks too soon. 'And I've got a whole hedge of it at Silver Birch Cottage.' It really was almost impossible not to feel the general happiness that always comes with the first really warm sunshine of the year. The birds were going crazy outside the wards, and their full-throated song cheered even the saddest of patients.

Tessa walked briskly along the corridor. She was slightly encouraged by Amy Moore's progress. She had eaten better this week, and her jaundice was clinically slightly better. Perhaps today's blood tests would confirm the improvement.

A tall, white-coated figure emerged from Ward Six. He almost collided with Tessa, as she hurried towards Seven. 'Oh, sorry.' He steadied her by holding her elbows. 'Hello, Tess.' Why did Adam always say her name as though it were the loveliest name in the world?

'Everything okay with you?' she asked.

He let go of her arms, slowly, reluctantly. 'Mustn't grumble.' He looked into her eyes then, and laughed, rather awkwardly. 'Hell, what a banal thing to say to you! What I mean is—there's no development in Lorna's case. We're hoping we can talk it all out on Saturday. The Chairman of the Practitioner Committee will be coming.' He brushed back a lock of hair, which she noticed was needing cutting. He had got his worried look back, the look that had first stirred her sympathy and her interest when she had seen him across the village church. He touched her elbow. 'Say, about Saturday —there isn't much point in taking two cars?'

'No, true. I'll take you with pleasure.' She was businesslike, glad that her voice betrayed nothing but her usual confident assurance.

Adam nodded. 'See you, then.'

She had stood, watching him, watching his white coat flapping open until he turned the corner. She found herself remembering the time he had come to her door wearing only jeans, and she had noticed his perfect physique, those sturdy shoulders and rounded pectorals. It was only what any trained doctor would notice, she thought. And then she had brushed at her eyes, which were unaccountably stinging as her vision clouded.

'Everything all right, Dr Daley?'

It was Staff Nurse Burrows, pushing a wheelchair

patient back to OP from X-Ray. 'Yes, thanks. Lovely morning, Nurse Burrows.'

'Great, isn't it?' The plump figure continued on her way, carefully manipulating the corner with the wheel-chair. Tessa nodded to herself. Great, it certainly was. Except that she was such a loser—first Guy, then Adam. She looked idly out of the window. Adam had helped her get over Guy—by showing her all the things she enjoyed that Guy would have hated. She must be grateful to him for that. And she had known he was tied up with Lorna from the very first day, so it was ridiculous to blame him for her falling for him so stupidly.

Her bleep went, startling her into movement from her reverie. She took a phone from the nearest wall-set. 'Yes? Daley here.'

'Ward Seven, Doctor. Can you come urgently?'

Tessa went into the ward. 'Sister? What's the problem?'

'It's Mrs Moore, Doctor. She can't get her breath.' Sister led the way to the bed, which was surrounded by its floral curtains. Sandy Singh stood by the bed, his stethoscope dangling from his hand. Tessa looked at Amy Moore's face. It was certainly less yellow, but just now it was twisted with pain as the poor woman struggled for breath.

Tessa hastily listened to her chest, then looked up at Sandy. 'Pneumothorax?' She listened again to both lungs. 'There seems to be air in both sides, but the left is the worst. Have you got a water-seal drainage bottle?'

'I brought it.' Sister had a trolley beside the bed, and she picked up a sterile hypodermic. 'Is this bore wide enough, Doctor?'

Tessa examined the needle. 'Yes, thank you.' She pointed to the other side of the bed. Sandy and Sister

Jones took up their places on each side of the patient, as
Tessa gently felt for the intercostal space, inserting the
needle with a deft stroke and pushing it down till she felt
it go into the pleural cavity. 'Tubing, please.' Sister had
placed it ready, and the student nurse handed it to her,
as she disengaged the hypodermic and attached the
tubing to the needle. 'Get this in the water, Sandy.'
Tessa gave the rubber tube to the houseman, who
attached it to a tube in the cork of a large water bottle on
the floor beside the bed. At once the little bubbles
showed that the unwanted air was flowing from the lung
space.

Tessa was attending to the other end of the tube in
Amy's chest. Sister Jones gently wiped the pale forehead, as Tessa put a wide round pad close to the skin,
and covered it with strapping, to hold it firmly in place.
Amy's breathing was better, but she was still slightly
blue around her lips. Tessa stayed beside her until it was
clear that the air was being drawn off, and her breathing
was improving. Amy's eyes closed with exhaustion, as
Tessa listened to her chest again. 'She's only sleeping,
but keep an eye on her, Nurse, and call someone if
there's any change.'

They left the poor woman with her curtains still drawn
around her. Sister provided a welcome cup of coffee as
they sat in the office, discussing the case. 'I've never
known a spontaneous pneumothorax in liver failure.'
Tessa shook back her hair, which was damp with sweat.
'I'd better have a word with the thoracic surgeons, in
case this doesn't clear up. This isn't really a rheumatology problem any more.'

Sister nodded. 'And her Caesar stitches are due out,
but I wasn't going to meddle until you gave the go-
ahead.'

'Oh, poor little Amy!' Tessa's brow was furrowed as she leaned her head on her hand. 'Is she going to make it after all this?'

Sandy said, 'Yesterday she was looking much better. The whites of her eyes were almost normal. And now —we almost lose her. What else can we do, Tessa?'

Tessa tried to be brisk. 'Test her blood again. Have a word with the surgeons. And pray.'

Sandy smiled ruefully. 'Yes, that I have already done. The husband has been to see the baby, Paula. He said she's the loveliest child he's ever seen.'

Tessa was silent. She was suddenly thinking of holding a tiny new baby in her arms. She had never felt the yearning before. Suddenly she realised that she would soon be too old to have children. It had never bothered her a scrap before, but now she felt unbearably sad for a moment, both for the young woman who was fighting for her life—and for herself, and the hurt of not knowing how it felt to hold her own child in her arms.

That night, something made Tessa telephone Gloria. 'How was Benidorm?' she asked.

'Gloriously hot, darling. I'm the most gorgeous shade of bronze, and it goes beautifully with the new white linen skirt I bought from Harrods this morning. But it's been jolly nice here, hasn't it, dear? Though I expect you haven't had much time for sunbathing.'

'No, Gloria, but I have been house-hunting. I've bought myself a cottage. Do bring Laura and come and see it soon. There's not an awful lot of room. In fact it's tiny—but very sweet. I love it.'

'Oh dear!' There was a short silence. 'Does that mean you're settling down up there?'

'Afraid so. But it isn't the North Pole, Gloria.'

Again a silence. 'But where on earth do you shop?'

Tessa smiled to herself. She was seeing Gloria so much more clearly now. 'To be honest, I don't need much. I have enough clothes for what I need.'

'And the—er—cottage? Have you furnished it?'

'I have, Gloria—there's a scruffy little town called Blackwood near here, where there's a shop called Kennedy Carpets. They did me proud—including a little Indian rug for the sitting-room for a lot less than Harrods.'

'Oh dear!' Gloria said again. Tessa could imagine Gloria's lip curling in a grimace of distaste. Then she said, her voice strangely distant, 'Guy would never have settled away from London.'

When Tessa put the phone down, she felt a strange sense of peace come over her. Gloria was quite right. She had done her a good turn, by emphasising what she already knew in her heart now—that Guy had not been right for her. They had shared some good times, some city times. But he would have been bored here. There would have been little for him to do. Tessa had her work—and was glad of the peace and quiet when she got home.

If she had married Guy, he would soon have come to hate her and her newly acquired love of the country. They would have parted, sooner or later. Tessa stared out from her hospital room that she would soon be leaving. She gazed out, but saw nothing. She felt greatly thankful that they had never reached the stage of any bitterness or recrimination. He had died a happy man, never knowing disappointment or anticlimax. Her memories of him would always be fond ones, unclouded by disillusion.

The setting sun was sending long shadows of the trees across the fields, and across the hospital car park. The sky was a luminous pink, shading gradually into turquoise and then to blue, deep cloudless blue. A jet flew across the sky, too high to be heard, leaving a trail of vapour that lingered, hovered, then slowly disintegrated, leaving the sky pure and clear again. Tessa looked up, and whispered, 'Goodbye, dear Guy.'

As she leaned her chin on her hands, drinking in the peace and the gentle chirrup of the birds, a man strode across the car park. It was Adam, dressed in light slacks and a white and brown patterned sweater. He opened the door of his silver BMW under the leafy oak tree. He flung his jacket into the back seat and got in, and she heard the engine start. She was leaning on both elbows, and it was too late to hide, as he suddenly lowered the window, put his head through and smiled at her. He raised his right hand from the wheel to give her a wave, and Tessa lifted hers in reply, as he drove away without looking back. There was no need to wonder where he was going.

For goodness' sake, get married quickly and buzz off to America, Forrester! Then we can get back to some normal life around here . . . She thought she had shaken him from all her thoughts. But all the same, she didn't get to sleep that night until long after she had heard him coming up the stairs, two at a time. She heard his door close. She heard him go to the bathroom. She heard him clean his teeth, and walk into the bedroom . . . She heard the click as his lamp went off.

On Saturday morning she woke early, because it was the day she was going to the Goodisons', and she wanted to wash her hair. It had grown very long now. She dried it, and tied it up in a ponytail. Ought she to drive into Blackwood and have something done to it? She could lunch at Potters, and have a natter with Joyce Ainsley. She wanted some information about what vegetables to plant in her own little garden, and Joyce's Stan was the man to advise her. Yes, the sun was bright, and a lazy day like that would be restful before the ordeal of dinner with Adam and the Goodisons . . .

There was a gentle, almost tentative tap at the door, and she walked over to open it, not really expecting Adam. And yet—'Have you had breakfast?' he asked, his voice giving nothing away.

'I—' she cleared her throat. Why did her voice fail when she tried to wish him good morning? 'Yes. A cup of tea and a vitamin tablet.' She stood back, gesturing him to come in. 'Do you want to make arrangements for tonight? I'm driving, aren't I?'

He nodded, and took a step inside. 'You look very pretty.'

She looked down at her white jeans and embroidered blue blouse. 'This is nothing.' A touch of wickedness crept into her voice. 'Wait till you see my outfit for tonight. I'm going to take hours getting ready, and I'm going to paint every inch of my face. You'll see—I'll be a knockout!' She smiled at him, trying to get through his wall of diffidence that stood between them. She wanted him to see that they could still be friends, even though he was an engaged man. She was rewarded by a trace of his old smile.

'That's nothing new,' he told her.

'What isn't?'

'You always are a knockout. Will you come for a walk with me?'

Tessa regarded him warily. 'What kind of walk?'

'One where you put one foot in front of the other.'

'That sounds reasonable. Only I haven't got all day

—and last time you shot off to the Pennines when we went for a walk.'

He shook his head. 'Not the Pennines. But it's too nice to stay in, and I'm not seeing Lorna till tonight. Will you?'

She hesitated. She wanted to, and Adam obviously wanted her to. 'I think I'd love to.' A walk was innocent enough.

'Come on, then.'

'Now?'

'This minute. Got your key?' She made sure it was in her shoulder-bag, then she followed him out, banging the door behind them.

They got in the BMW. 'Is Lorna working this morning?' Tessa queried.

He started the engine, looking sideways at her. 'That isn't why I asked you.'

'Don't get on the defensive, man! It's only a question.'

'Sorry. No, she isn't working at all. Old Blake has got a locum—Lorna needed some leave while all this was going on. And if the locum likes the place, he'll stay on.'

Tessa felt a heaviness in her heart—though it was only what she expected. This was the first step to preparations for going to America. A replacement partner for Dr Blake—of course. Lorna couldn't leave him single-handed. Now they could go to the States together, and take the exam that all foreign-qualified doctors must sit. Then she could set up a lucrative practice in the best part of Washington, while Adam took up his professorship. It all made sense.

He said, 'You're very deep in thought.'

'I'm sorry.' She sat up, and looked out of the window. They had already passed through Blackwood, making for the M6 up North. 'Hey, where are we going?'

'For a walk.'

'I know.' She looked at him accusingly. 'It's the Pennines again.'

'No, another of my favourite places—Crummock.'

'Where's that?'

He smiled. 'It's one of the loveliest places in the world.'

'I said where, not what.' Then she asked, 'If it's so lovely, why didn't you ask Lorna to go with you?'

'I—She doesn't like walking.' Adam negotiated the turn to the slip road to the motorway. The traffic was fairly brisk, but Adam soon made his way through to the fast lane, where he allowed the smooth engine to open out, to purr its way along as though they were floating on air.

It didn't seem long before Tessa realised where Crummock was. They shot past a sign that read 'The Lakes.' 'Adam, you're going to the Lake District!'

'I am, I am, I admit it.'

'You might have said!'

'You wouldn't have come,' he pointed out.

'You're right.'

'Want to go back?'

'No.'

'That's good, because I think you'll enjoy it. It's time you got out more, saw some real scenery. You townees think a walk in St James' Park is communing with nature!'

Tessa laughed. 'I'm no townee, man, I'm an Elderton landowner. I'm a countrywoman now. I suppose the next thing I'll do is join the Women's Institute.' Then she put her hand over her mouth. 'I ought not to have mentioned that—I'm sorry.'

'Don't be. Lorna has pulled out of these things anyway. She was never any good at making chutney, or knitting rugs.' It was nice of him to make a joke of it, but she ought not to have said anything that implied criticism of his fiancée. It wasn't good form.

'She's given up her activities, then?' she queried.

'Yes. She's keeping a low profile for the moment. It seems best, until this affair has blown over.'

'You think it will, then?'

'I hope so. There's a good chance.' Adam took his eyes from the road for a second and met her look. 'Now, no more talk of the case. Look out of the window, Tess, and don't miss a moment. It's worth it, I promise.'

She wanted him to talk about Lorna, but if he was unwilling, then she might as well do as he suggested, and admire the scenery. Half her mind was reluctant at first, but soon she almost gasped with delight, as the motorway rounded a corner, and great rolling hills began to rise from the hazy blue-green fields and hedgerows. White lambs pranced and danced beside proud mothers. The hills were blue, tipped with snow left over from the winter. After a while Tessa ceased to speak at all, drinking in the beauty as though drunk, overwhelmed by delight in the abundance of perfection.

They passed through some small grey stone towns. Adam drew up at a roadside inn at about eleven, and they had coffee sitting at the door under a gay umbrella, gazing out over moors and hills. He told her the names of the crags around then, knowing them off by heart. 'Why do we need to go any further, Adam?' queried Tessa. 'It's so lovely here.'

'I'd like to show you Honister. I used to camp here with my school friends. Then when I was a student, a few of us did some rock climbing on Gable and Helvellyn.'

'Why did you stop?'

'Work, mainly. You know there are no long holidays once a medical student starts working in hospitals. There never seems time.'

'I suppose you were ambitious to get your exams done? Get Primary first time, did you?'

He nodded, smiling. 'Yes, you mean I was a swot?'

'No, no. You have to work hard if you want to get proper satisfaction from the job.' Tessa looked across the little wooden table, admiring his rugged handsomeness against a backdrop of rolling new bracken and grazing sheep. She was beginning to feel comfortable with him, beginning to feel the attraction that she thought she had conquered. She tried not to wish Lorna Goodison didn't exist. 'How old are you?' she asked.

'Thirty-six.'

'How did you escape being married so long?'

His eyes were amused. 'I always thought marriage wasn't for me. Some of my student friends married young, and somehow they always seemed to be arguing about little things, and it took the edge off for me.'

'And now?'

'I still think marriage hasn't changed. Only when you meet someone special, it makes you re-think a bit.' He drained his coffee cup. 'Come on, you've grilled me enough. Come and tell me your life story as we go over the Honister Pass.'

The car began to climb. The narrow road wound round, zigzagging up the mountainside. Tessa couldn't control her gasps of delight at the tumbling beck that skipped and bounced its way down the hillside in noisy waterfalls and sparkling pools, under the dappled shade of beech trees in early fresh green, and catkins, dangling and swinging like the tails of the baby lambs.

They came out of the shade into bright sunlight, as the

pass wound between two great moors. Adam pressed a button, and the sun-roof swished back, so that the warmth of the sun and the sound of the birds were sensed more clearly. 'I'm glad you like it,' he said softly, watching Tessa's face for a moment.

They had started the downward journey now, passing through more rocks, and beside a slate quarry. The beck had become a meandering river. Then Tessa's breath was taken away by the sudden appearance of a blue lake, sparkling in the sun, surrounded by craggy peaks, still streaked with snow, reflected deep below in the still blue water. 'Adam, how perfect!' she exclaimed. And as they neared the lake, he stopped at the side of the road for her to drink in the immense view all around her. 'Adam, leave me here. I never want to be anywhere else!'

She did not see the gentle look in his eyes, or even notice that his arm was along the back of her seat. But somehow they were close together, and her head seemed to rest quite naturally on his shoulder, just because they had to sit close to see the two white swans that padded into view as though pulled by strings. They stopped, their graceful necks bent, mirrored in the still water as though admiring their own beauty.

Then Adam gave Tessa's shoulder a squeeze. 'Come on, love, we'll leave the car here. We'll have lunch at the Fish and walk a little way round the lake. Pity we have to go to the Goodisons', there's a splendid walk all round Buttermere.' If Tessa had been listening properly she would have detected a distinct note of irritation at the thought of going to the Goodisons'. But she wasn't listening, unable to take in everything at the same time.

'Will we have left by sunset? It must seem like Paradise here.' She followed him down the path and across some springy short grass. A black lamb scampered out of their way. 'Everything smells so pure!'

'I knew you'd like it. It refreshes the soul and the senses.' He looked at her with his dark blue eyes, and for a moment she forgot that he belonged to someone else, and smiled back as though they were friends, and always would be. 'Just like you,' he added softly.

Tessa tried to pretend she hadn't heard. She turned and strode out over the grass again. 'When you're across the world in America, you can think of me driving up here, and remembering the first time I was brought, on such a lovely day,' she told him.

'I daresay I will—think of you sometimes.' His voice sounded sad. But he couldn't be sad, surely? He was the one who had chosen to leave for America; no one was forcing him.

'Don't order much,' warned Adam as they sat at a small table by a window with a half pint of cider each. 'There'll be at least seven courses at the Goodisons'.'

After lunch they walked by Buttermere and across the patch of spongy grass to Crummock Water. Halfway, their hands brushed together, and Adam took hers in his. She felt a shiver go through her. Yet it seemed natural at that moment, and she made no protest, but rather clung on to his hand like a child, feeling safe, and untroubled, as though this lovely moment of time was separated from the rest of the world. They stood at the water's edge, shaded by the trees, the water sparkling like jewels. It was achingly beautiful. Tessa felt deeply the tragedy of loss in the middle of perfection. They avoided one another's gaze after that, and she wondered if Adam read her thoughts, as he had done before.

They drove back almost in silence, still under the spell of the place. 'I think we may be a bit late,' Adam said.

'But fortunately you only take a short while to get ready, don't you?'

She tried to tease him. 'Oh, Adam, you know women? I've got my hair to style, and my toenails to varnish. And I haven't decided which earrings to wear. And I thought of having a go with the eyeliner tonight. If the eyeliner goes wrong, do you know you have to start the make-up all over again?'

He took her up. 'In that case, if you've got so much to do, I'll just have to put my foot down.' And he pushed the car faster, so that they began to pass all on the road with a whoosh. Tessa didn't protest, seeing that the motorway was getting crowded, and knowing he couldn't keep up such a speed.

It was just after seven when they drew up under the oak tree. 'It's a good job you're taking me tonight,' said Adam, 'I'm almost out of petrol.'

'How many miles have we done?'

He checked the instrument. 'Two hundred and fifty.'

'Wow!' Tessa climbed out of the car.

'Tess—' he began.

'Yes?'

'I love—loved today.'

'I loved it too. Every second.' She turned away quickly. As Adam turned to lock the car door, she noticed on the ground the withered little rosebud she had thrown out of the window. She looked round. Adam was not watching her. Swiftly she bent and picked it up, then she said casually, 'Meet me by the Metro in twenty minutes,' and ran inside.

She was glowing with the beauty of the day. She showered quickly with scented soap. There was no time at all to bother with make-up, to do her nails, even to try out more than one dress. She selected the first formal gown she reached in the wardrobe, then she brushed her hair till it shone, and inserted some tiny drop-pearl earrings. With a quick squirt of her best Chanel perfume, she twirled once in front of the mirror, and was ready.

The rosebud lay where she had put it on the coffee table, brown and crushed. Tessa stopped and picked it up gently, then bent and kissed it. 'Sorry,' she whispered, and put it back in the glass jug with some fresh water. Then she shook her head at her own silliness. Dead things don't come back to life.

CHAPTER ELEVEN

'To think I was one of those who thought we ought to restrict the intake of women into our medical schools!' Dr Fielding was the Chairman of the local Family Practitioner Committee. He meant it as a compliment, as he came into the Goddisons' sumptuous drawing room before dinner with his host, Daniel Goodison. Tessa was sitting beside Lorna, after she and Adam had been indulging in some very reticent small talk, hedging round the subject they had all come to discuss.

Lorna was subdued tonight, and it added to her beauty. But she was the first to take up her guests' rather chauvinistic remark. 'I'm sure you're paying our guest a compliment, Dr Fielding,' she said sweetly.

'Both of you, Dr Goodison, both of you. Come, Daniel, we're lucky men to have such attractive company.'

Tessa stood up to be introduced. After shaking his hand, she said demurely to Dr Fielding, 'You disapprove of women doctors, then?'

'No, no. Only that half of them leave to get married. Men ought to have priority, don't you think?'

'Half of them?' Lorna rose like a queen to Tessa's side. 'I wonder how accurate your figures are? As far as I know, all the women who trained with me are working.'

Tessa nodded. 'I agree. I was at our university reunion last year, and I didn't meet anyone who had given up, or even taken a part-time job. Some had young families.

161

But they had taken maternity leave, and then gone straight back into productive medical work.'

Dr Fielding, to give him credit, was quick to apologise. 'I must train my old brain to accept that pretty women are as likely to be efficient as good-looking men. Forgive me—I plead age, and a certain dryness of the throat—oh, thank you, Daniel.' Mr Goodison was handing round champagne. Tessa resumed her seat, wondering who was going to start the business part of the evening. She noticed that Adam sat close to Lorna, and she had to admit to herself that they made a superb couple, both so strikingly handsome. Lorna wore a loose-sleeved dress in pure leaf-green silk, that set off her chestnut hair, newly set in a bouffant style around a perfectly made-up face. Her eyebrows were arched and delicately drawn. Her lashes were flicked up with a mascara that contained a hint of dark green, that emphasised her large and lovely eyes.

Suddenly she realised that she was being spoken to. 'Tuesday.' She looked up quickly, to see Daniel Goodison at her side. 'It's arranged, then?'

'Yes, Dr Daley. Tuesday at ten-thirty.'

Lorna said across the room, 'Yes, Tessa—I face my judges.' She gave a little laugh, but it was then that Tessa saw the lines of worry at the corners of her mouth, and the single frown line that even the best make-up could not hide.

Tessa said quickly, 'It's not the guillotine, Lorna.'

'I hope not.' Lorna took another glass of champagne. Tessa wondered how many times Lorna had been baled out of trouble by her proud and doting father. Only now did she realise that Daddy could do very little. Tessa caught the glitter of the diamond on Lorna's finger. With a man like Adam Forrester beside her, Lorna would soon get over whatever the local committee and Jack Crowe could throw at her.

'When are you moving in to be our next-door neighbour, Dr Daley?'

'Wednesday. I'm taking three days off to finish hemming my curtains and attend to all the loose ends.' She didn't go on about her home. It was private, all the plans she had made—her vegetable garden, her arch of climbing roses over the gate, her honeysuckle, and the Siamese kitten she planned to buy.

Adam Forrester said, 'Tess, you look like a cat with cream. You must be very pleased with the cottage.'

She nodded. She had hoped it didn't show, her new delight in being alone, away from disturbances like other women's fiancés. But now she had admitted it, she made a joke of it. 'I'll try not to be a nuisance, Mr Goodison. At least you know there's no room to hold wild parties!'

The smiling host stood up. 'There's no one else I'd have liked better for a neighbour.' For a moment, Tessa felt a warning note at the back of her mind. Daniel Goodison was indeed taking a lot of interest in her. She thought it was because he was making sure she was on Lorna's side in the hearing. But there might be another reason—a lonely widower, whose only daughter was soon going away . . . and a single woman, possibly lonely too . . . living most conveniently close . . . Tessa was appalled at her own thoughts, and hastily put them from her mind. She didn't want to offend Mr Goodison. She must make sure they did not become too friendly.

Dinner was really as good as Adam had promised. They had a woman who helped in the kitchen, but most of the dishes had been cooked by Lorna herself, and though Tessa hated to admit it, had been cooked very well indeed.

'The salmon was beautiful, Lorna,' she smiled.

'Thank you, but it's my fishmonger you must praise. I'll let you have a list of some of the good shops at this end of town.'

'Thank you, I'd like that. Though entertaining isn't one of my talents, I have to admit.'

'Then you can sit in your own little kitchen and spoil yourself.' Lorna and Tessa had by now become almost friends with the help of the delicious meal. Her hostess leaned over and said privately to Tessa, 'You know, I do know what kind of mistakes I've made. You were quite right. You've helped me to make a big change in myself, but the worry is to convince the Committee of this change.'

Tessa nodded wisely. She knew very well that Lorna was buttering her up, just like her father was. 'Do you want to talk about it now?' she asked.

Lorna shook her head, then stood up, followed at once by the men. 'I think we'll have our coffee in the drawing-room, Daddy.'

Dr Fielding leaned across to Tessa. 'Then if we have ours in Daniel's study, we can get the nitty-gritty over before the liqueurs, Dr Daley.'

'Certainly.' They were both shown to a small panelled room filled with bookcases and some eighteenth-century landscapes in heavy gilt frames.

'Will you sit here, Dr Daley?' Dr Fielding offered her a gilt satin chair that looked as though it had come from Buckingham Palace. He was a handsome old man, with delicate silver hair and a kindly patrician face. 'You know I'm—er—"defending" in this case? It's not a good term, but it means I put forward Lorna's side of the case.'

'I understand. But do you mind if I say at once that I

won't jump through any hoops at Mr Goodison's sugges-- tion? I will not say, or put my name to, anything inaccurate or circumspect.'

The old man nodded sagely. The housekeeper came in then with a silver tray and coffee service, and they did not speak while she poured their coffee into exquisite china cups. When the door had closed behind her, he said, 'Yes, my dear—may I call you Tessa?—you've gained that reputation. That's why he asked you. Your support of Lorna would be most valuable in her defence.'

Tessa felt her unhappiness grow. 'But, Dr Fielding, this isn't just a question of right and wrong. Hundreds of people in Foxleigh and Blackwood must have heard of this inquiry. Even if nothing is proved, rumours go on, don't they, Doctor?'

He took a sip of coffee, added more sugar, and stirred it well before he went on. 'Ah, but it isn't the rumours we're dealing with. We're investigating only one com- plaint—that of Jack Crowe against Lorna Goodison because of her failure to treat Mother Crowe in good time.'

'How is Mother Crowe?' asked Tessa.

'She died two days ago.'

'Poor old lady!'

'Do you really think so, Tessa? Isn't it better for her to slip away with no pain than to linger? I'm sure Jack Crowe will think so, when his anger subsides.' The old man leaned forward. 'Some of his anger is really against himself—his own guilt for not visiting his mother often enough. You've met this type of guilt?'

'Yes, I have.' Dr Fielding was quite right. Yet he was also very clever at putting the case. Lorna was lucky to have such a bright defender. Tessa looked around at the room, the subtle gold touches on the graceful ceiling mouldings. Would Adam use this room, before they emigrated? She put her hand to her head, wishing she were out of the whole business, wishing she could control her dreadful, overpowering love for him. It almost frightened her, the obsession for him that pulsed through her, whatever she was doing, whatever else she was trying to think about.

Dr Fielding misinterpreted her gesture. 'My dear Tessa, I'm truly sorry that you have to go through this. All I want is your permission to use a statement from you.'

Tessa sat up. She had to be honest. 'Please don't tell anyone outside this room, but I have two patients who've suffered because of Lorna Goodison's negligence—yes, negligence! They've suffered pain, joint damage, and possibly permanent disability!'

Dr Fielding sat back, his face solemn. 'I see.'

Tessa felt mean. 'I know she took on too many commitments—and has given them up now. Her medical competence and dedication, I believe, have improved already. But who's to prove this?'

'Well, you could help—by giving her a chance.' His voice was quiet and gentle.

'I could say I believed she was better, but a clever lawyer could easily question me about other cases. There's no defence against the truth, Doctor.'

Dr Fielding stood up and faced her, his hands behind his back. 'I'm now a clever lawyer, Tessa, and I'm about to question you on the specific case here before me.' He paused, and looked out of the window for a moment. The dusky lawn stretched as far as they could see before darkness stopped their view of the poplars at the edge of the garden. 'Dr Daley, what would you say to the question of diagnosis of carcinoma of the pancreas?'

'Well, it's not straightforward—there are often no physical signs in the early stages. Apart from testing blood, only laparotomy would prove anything conclusive. And there has, in my experience anyway, usually to be a history of alcohol intake. I understand Mother Crowe never drank.'

'So you wouldn't have sent Mother Crowe for laparotomy?'

'No. Blood tests, yes.'

'At the first visit?'

Tessa thought. 'It depends on her complaints. I might have sent her away with a prescription for antacids at the first visit, but with a proviso that she return in a couple of weeks if no better.'

'Exactly. That's what Lorna did. The old woman claimed she felt much better, and didn't return until much later.' Dr Fielding sat down again. 'More coffee, my dear?' The interview appeared to be over. He refilled their cups.

'Is that it?' asked Tessa.

He smiled over his cup. 'In your opinion as a general physician, the diagnosis is difficult. We might almost say, often missed at first?'

'I'm afraid we might almost say that,' she agreed.

'And the outcome is always fatal, whether diagnosed or not?'

'In time, yes.'

'So had Mrs Crowe's cancer been diagnosed earlier, she might still have died two days ago?'

'You win, Dr Fielding. I have to agree that in this case, if cancer had been found, and the pancreas removed, she might have spent six months on a drip in hospital—and still have died two days ago.' Tessa waved her hand to stop him interrupting. 'Yes, Doctor, I *would* rather go as she did—happy and living a normal life until almost the end.'

They both drank their coffee, a sense of completeness stealing over Tessa. She had been totally honest, yet Dr Fielding seemed satisfied. He said, 'Shall we join the others?'

'Very well.'

'I won't ask you to appear, Tessa, but if I may, I'll use your name. The Committee will have a general discussion on all aspects of the case, and Lorna will be available if they wish to question her. But you—you couldn't really call yourself a close friend of the accused, can you?'

Tessa gave a wry smile. A friend? Of the woman who was marrying Adam? It was impossible. She said mildly, 'No, we don't know each other very well,' and wondered at her own acting ability.

They walked slowly along the thick-carpeted corridor towards the drawing-room. Dr Fielding said quietly, 'I think the case will be dismissed.'

'Good. It hasn't been pretty.'

He nodded. 'Village life can be very cruel. Everyone knows everything—and distorts it, more often than not.' They were at the door. He said quietly, 'Lorna has already resigned from our area anyway, so the other members won't think it a problem requiring much attention.' He twinkled slightly, like a gnome under the wall light. 'I rather think her resignation has more to do with a certain wealthy young man, rather than with John Crowe.'

'Her marriage, you mean?' queried Tessa.

'Certainly. She wouldn't want to stay here when her husband is miles away, now, would she? She's lucky to have him. And she's also lucky to have your backing, my dear. Thank you very much.'

'Don't thank me. I would have said the same for anyone.' Tessa spoke in a low voice, for they were right outside the drawing-room door now. 'I just have a thing about unfairness, I have to fight it. Maybe I'll mellow with age, and accept life for what it is.'

He held out his hand and shook hers warmly. 'I'm sure your life will be blessed, Tessa.'

'Thank you.' She smiled, and whispered, 'Don't you feel a bit like a guest at a Buckingham Palace garden party?'

He grinned, and answered with another whisper. 'Don't be overawed. Daniel's father bought this place with the profits from a lifetime in the wholesale meat business!' He said no more. Whoever those weighty portraits were, they were certainly not Goodisons. Tessa and Dr Fielding were both smiling broadly as they entered the room.

Lorna stood up and crossed the room to meet them. 'What have you decided?' she asked anxiously.

Dr Fielding said gently, 'I believe the Committee will go along with my argument that in Mrs Crowe's case, it was a difficult diagnosis.'

'Oh, I do hope so.' She turned to Tessa, her eyes sincere. 'You've been so very kind. I have a lot to thank you for.' She squeezed Tessa's hand, then ran back into Adam's arms, where he held her, until she regained her composure. Tessa turned away, to receive Daniel Goodison's thanks.

Tessa felt suddenly very weary. 'I really must go,' she said.

'So soon? Ah, well, when we're neighbours, you'll pop in a lot, I hope.'

'Most kind.' Tessa had no intention of popping any-where. She wanted to get away from here—if Adam wanted a lift, he would have to disentangle himself from Lorna's loving arms. Tessa couldn't bear to see them so openly in love, and she turned away, keeping her good-byes as brief as possible. She knew she had given Lorna peace of mind. It had been in her power to refuse, but what good would it have done? Only made her feel guilty for being childish. She gave her peace of mind willingly. It was Adam Forrester that she would never have given up, had she the chance. She would have wound herself round him like the ivy that encircled the oak tree in the car park, together for ever . . .

Tessa said to Adam, 'Sorry to rush off. I'll wait in the car while you say goodbye to Lorna.' She shook hands with Dr Fielding and Daniel Goodison, and hurried across the gravel drive into the car.

Adam, however, was tapping at the other door before she had time to unlock it. 'I've said goodbye,' he said, settling himself in and pulling down the seatbelt. Tessa looked at him in surprise. For someone so recently embracing his true love, he sounded almost relieved to get away. She drove back along the quiet country road. They met no other traffic, and she had to brake while a couple of stoats ran lissomely across the road in the beam from her headlights.

'You tired?' she asked.

'Fairly. I'm very grateful to you, Tess love. It means so much.'

'You've been the one to help her. I only hope she never forgets that, as long as she lives. She owes you everything.' And Tessa choked back any more words, in case they betrayed her emotion and welled up and threatened to intrude into the impersonal conversation she was trying so hard to maintain.

They walked up the stairs of the doctors' flats together, but not touching. Adam said as they stopped at his door, 'This must be one of the longest days of your life, Tess—not counting housemanship, of course.' He touched her arm. 'You're worn out. It was selfish of me to drag you all that way this morning.'

The night seemed very quiet. She could hear his clock ticking behind the closed door. She said, 'Just the opposite,' and her eyes brightened at the memory. 'Without that wonderful first part, I don't think I could have stuck the last part. Thank you for that, Adam.'

She turned to go, but he said, 'Wait a moment.'

'Yes?' She faced him again.

'I was wondering—you seem—to have got over Guy—?'

She wasn't offended. 'Yes, I think so.'

'Maybe getting your cottage helped?'

'Yes, I'm sure it did,' she agreed.

'Is there anything I can do to help when you move?'

She smiled. 'Adam, you've got a full list—I saw the lists for Wednesday. But don't worry, I'll invite you and Lorna for a drink when I'm straight.' She patted his shoulder, for she was on the next step up, and her eyes were on a level with his navy blue ones, shadowed in the dim light. Then she turned and ran quickly up, without saying good night.

She wished she had not made that invitation. Once she left this little flat, she wanted it to be a clean break with Adam too. She did not put the light on, but went across to the window and opened it. The air was still soft and warm for April. The fields and forests were now white with a frosting of moonlight, and the moon hung like some crystal ball exuding silver beams. Tessa smiled.

The first time she had stared through this window, her heart had been heavy, and she had lost her one true love. Now she could smile at herself, as she knew her heart was almost equally heavy at losing Adam. The difference was that she was sad, but not depressed. Although her heart was empty, yet she was full of hope and optimism. Her life could still be busy and constructive. She might never hold a child of her own in her arms, but with a job like hers she could help dozens of children, and that would be a reward almost as good.

She slept more soundly than she had done for years, allowing the memories of the lakes and mountains she had seen for the first time that day to dominate her last thoughts. And she woke with the feeling of optimism still strong. It was Sunday. Of course—it was Easter Sunday. That was why Lorna's inquiry had to be on the Tuesday. She would go to church today, and then arrange all her few possessions into neat piles, for the removal men to take on Wednesday. There would also be time for another visit to the cottage, to see how the alterations had progressed.

It must have been the most heavenly Easter weather for years. As Tessa walked up the winding church path she recalled how she had first walked it, treading heedlessly on damp, autumn-smelling leaves, the feeling of death and depression still heavy in her heart. Now she looked with delight at the borders of budding crocuses, the neatly mown grass, and the trees in bold new leaf. She no longer walked alone; the villagers, smiling at the sunshine, and dressed in their new outfits, greeted her as an old friend. She saw Joyce and Stan there, with Jennet in a sweet straw hat, looking mature and pretty. Sharon and Kenneth Billington were near the front, and they

waved when they saw her. She sat nearer the front than
on that first grey day, when she had crept in, like some
waif, and sat in the back pew.

It was only after the service, when the little congregation had sung its heart out to the wheezy old organ,
that Tessa noticed Adam going out in front of her. In
contrast to the relaxed mood of the others, his handsome
face looked tense again. He shook hands with Mr
Appleby, the vicar, then with a quick nod he made off
down the path, not speaking to anyone else, as though
his mind was on other things.

Tessa was wearing a dusty pink linen suit, with a
cream silk blouse and pretty matching pink shoes. She
drove along to the Brown Cow because she intended to
go along to the cottage, after a sandwich and a glass of
brown ale. Otherwise she would have walked, drinking
in the warmth of a perfect day. She drew into the inn car
park.

'Excuse me.'

Tessa turned as she got out of the car. A very pretty
dark woman stood there, beside a small sports car.
'Good morning—lovely morning,' Tessa greeted
her.

'Yes, it's beautiful. Could you tell me if this is the only
pub in the village?'

Tessa surveyed the petite figure, dressed in a grey
pleated skirt and lemon yellow top. She was very smart
—and not from round here. 'Yes, it's Foxleigh's only
pub. Are you meeting someone?'

'I—I'm—not quite sure. Is the manager a Mr
Browne?'

The penny dropped. 'Why, you're Beth!'

The other woman looked startled, then a little
pleased. 'You know about me? You're a friend of

Sam's?' She looked at Tessa closely, and Tessa could read the suspicions forming in Beth's mind.

Tessa held out her hand. 'I'm Tessa Daley—I'm a doctor at the hospital. And yes, I am a friend of Sam's. And no, nothing more, I promise. There's only one woman in that man's life.' She watched Beth's face. She had been right: Beth had learnt the hard and bitter way that Sam was the man for her—if he'd still have her. She was thin, and her face, though sweet, bore dark rings round her eyes, showing how she had agonised over coming here. Tessa went on quickly, 'Come on in and get it over, Beth. You won't regret it.'

There was a mixture of feelings in the other woman's face. Beth had been scared that Sam had found someone else, and Tessa had reassured her about this. And Tessa knew that her own rather glamorous appearance had notched up a plus for Sam—if Tessa was his friend, then he must be still attractive to women. Beth took a deep breath, then nodded. 'I'd like to come in, but it might be too much of a shock.'

'Then wait here.' Tessa looked around her. The trees around the little car park were almost bridal, with their white and pink cherry blossom that was just beginning to open all around them. 'I'll send him out.' She went quickly into the bar.

Sam saw her coming, and as he drew the half pint of bitter for her he lifted his eyebrows in amazement. 'Spring has come! Tessa, you're a sight for sore eyes.'

She leaned over the bar and whispered, 'Happy Easter, Sam. There's a friend waiting in the car park. Go on, don't keep her waiting, she's come a long way.'

He knew what she meant, and his hand trembled as he put down the glass in front of her. He didn't speak, but smoothed back his bushy black locks nervously and edged round Annie Blunt to get out of the doorway. He turned once, and Tessa put her thumb in the air, then he was gone.

She was not surprised when Sam did not return. But the Blunt sisters loved being left in charge. Tessa ate her prawn sandwich, reflecting that they were probably in for a very busy day. It was impossible not to be delighted for Sam. She would miss him, and his bluff sympathy. But then she didn't need sympathy now, did she? She was planning a new life, and thoroughly enjoying the process.

'You're going to live in the witch's cottage, ain't you?'

Tessa was sitting in her usual corner. 'Yes, young Billy, I am. I've brought my own broomstick.'

He looked puzzled, unable to see her joke. She smiled, and said, 'Have a drink on me, Billy. I'm going to make that little cottage into a fairy palace.'

Annie brought him his shandy, and the young man shoved his tow-coloured hair back from his vacant blue eyes. Only now they showed some interest. 'Fairy palace?'

Tessa nodded. She could tell Billy; he would know she wasn't boasting. 'Yes. I want to get someone to build me an archway over the gate, then I'm planting climbing roses, pink and orange and yellow, so that they make a gorgeous entrance. And there'll be honeysuckle and clematis up the walls—when I get a trellis. And a bank of lavender near the door, so that going in and coming out will be lovely every day.' She smiled at him. 'Doesn't that sound great?'

'Oh yes. Oh yes!' His eyes were bright now. 'Let me make the archway! I'm good with me hands, honest.'

Annie, who had stayed to listen, unashamed, confirmed this at once. 'Aye, he is that. He fettled me dad's

fence something great, he did. He worked as a joiner's
apprentice once. He'd do you a good job.'

Tessa smiled. 'Then you're hired, Billy. I have no
wood yet, but we'll soon get round to that. I'll order the
roses right away, when I go into town on Tuesday.' Her
face darkened a little, as she thought of the ordeal
Lorna—and Adam and she herself—would be going
through on Tuesday morning. How lovely to be able to
forget it afterwards by ordering her roses!

'I've got a fair lot of bits,' said Billy. 'I'll come round
on me bike, and you show me what you'll be wanting.'

And so she spent Easter Sunday and Monday at Silver
Birch Cottage. Billy not only turned up with his joinery
tools, but with a hoe and some shears tied to his back.
His obsession with witches had been replaced with a
glorious vision of fairies, and as Tessa watched him work
through her little kitchen window, she saw him smiling
as though at invisible elves who had come to help him.
And the hawthorn hedge that edged the bottom of her
back garden was almost in flower, its sweet-smelling
white blossoms just beginning to open. It was a perfect
backcloth to the young man's simple fantasies. When
she took him a mug of tea, they sat together in the
garden and planned magnificent dreams together. Even
the sight of her besom didn't upset him. He took it at
once to sweep away some dead twigs he had pruned from
the hedge.

She came back to Foxleigh tired, but she was cheered
by the realisation that Adam Forrester had not entered
her mind for at least the past four hours. She was
obviously getting over her infatuation. Silver Birch
Cottage was the ideal prescription. 'You're not a bad
physician, old girl,' she said to herself, as she walked
wearily up the stairs, her feet dragging with tiredness.

She stopped with a delighted smile. Her little battered rosebud was blooming again!

It was a lovely evening. The sun had set in an explosion of fire, with flame-coloured beams lighting up the sky over the trees. A magpie flapped its way across the field and settled in the car park, on the oak tree, a chic and elegant sight.

One for sorrow? At that moment, a white Porsche drove into the park and Adam got out. He bent, and said something to Lorna. She reached up with her left hand, the diamond shining blood red in the rays of the sun, and pulled him down to kiss his lips gently. Tessa turned away, and tried not to lose her inner joy she thought she had caught for keeps.

The telephone rang. 'Doctor, I thought you ought to know—Mrs Moore has died.' Tessa sat on the bed. Slowly the dead feeling she thought had gone for ever began to clutch at her heart. One for sorrow. The tears overflowed, and dripped down her suntanned cheeks.

Somewhere in the blank greyness there were footsteps coming up the stairs. Then they stopped, and there was a long pause. Tessa sensed in the grey mist only the pale strained face of Amy Moore, struggling for breath.

'The door was open.'

She started, and looked up. Adam was there, his blue eyes dark and unreadable. She looked into his face—but there was nothing to say.

He crossed the floor between them in two strides and knelt at her feet. 'Tess love, what is it?' His fingers wiped at her tears, gentle and warm and thrilling. His voice was meltingly tender, his face concerned and boyish as he looked up at her. At any other time she could have held him close. That was what he wanted, she knew, as he softly stroked her cheek and searched her face with anxious eyes.

It was a cruel intrusion, into her private grief, where he did not belong and never could. Tessa herself could never hurt him. But it was as though something outside herself, taut, raw and overcoiled, snapped, and lashed out at him. 'Get out, for God's sake! Get out, damn you, before I scream the place down!'

He was on his feet at once, standing, strong yet distant, over her shaking form. She did not look up, could not face him. With one touch on her shoulder, a firm squeeze, he was gone. Tessa flung herself face downward on the bed as the door slammed behind him, grabbing the pillow to muffle her sobs.

CHAPTER TWELVE

THE Council Chamber where Lorna's inquiry was to be held was a squat, grey Victorian building, with a flight of steps to the imposing carved double doors. Tessa approached it with lead in her shoes. She knew she didn't have to come, but having stood by Lorna with her testimony, she felt she had to show her that her support was genuine. Though Adam Forrester was sure to be around.

Life was showing its true colours now, Tessa thought. Her brief glimpse of happiness and peace of mind had been upset last night. Both her personal life and her professional life had been severely hurt yet again. The death of Mrs Moore would have been tragic at any time, but coming straight after the sight of Lorna and Adam together, Tessa felt her heart had been given more than it was fair to stand.

She walked up the steps, through the doors, and looked around for some indication where to go next. Lorna Goodison was standing close to a closed door, in the right-hand corridor. She was alone. 'Lorna? Where's everyone?'

'Oh, Tessa!' Lorna's face was drawn and tense, her large eyes even more lustrous than usual with unshed tears. 'Thank you. Thank you so much for coming.' She half extended her arms, then retreated humbly. 'I'm so very glad to see you!'

'That's all right.' Tessa's kindly nature took pity, even on the woman who was taking Adam away. She leaned over and gave Lorna a quick hug. 'Where's Adam? And your father?'

'Adam's working. Anyway, he's done enough. He promised to stand by me, and he did.'

'He did indeed. But I would have thought he wanted to be here. Where's your father?'

'Daddy had to go to a conference at Smithfield. He's certain he's fixed everything. But Tessa, I feel so very bad,' Lorna confessed. 'Suppose it goes against me?'

'It won't.' But Tessa thought Lorna ought to have shown more penitence about the patients she had indeed treated with negligence. She ought to feel awful about them too. 'This has been a warning to you. Just make sure that never again can this charge be brought against you.'

'I will, I will.' Lorna walked up and down, petulantly. She wore a suit of dark grey, with a blouse of pale blue, and elegant black court shoes. Every inch a professional woman. 'I suppose this sort of thing has never happened to you?'

'Oh yes, it has. There are always patients who blame you when things go wrong. One man nearly attacked me when his wife died of a cerebral haemorrhage, and I hadn't even seen her. But I was on duty at the time, and he was distraught, so—I got it in the neck—literally.'

While they talked, Tessa found her mind wandering. Here she was, the only person to support Lorna with her presence, yet Lorna had just taken from her the only thing she prized in the world. It was ironic. 'Why don't we take a breath of fresh air, Lorna? It's pretty grim standing in this corridor—it smells of disinfectant.'

They walked down the steps and across the road, where there was a wooden bench for weary shoppers.

They sat down, while the pale sun came out from a bank of cloud that had threatened rain first thing. A woman limped past them, then stopped, and retraced her halting steps. It was Sharon Billington.

'Hello, Dr Daley, I'm so glad to see you. You were right, you know. Being pregnant is keeping my aches and pains away something champion. I feel like a new woman!'

'That's good, Sharon.' Tessa had stood up, and she moved to one side so that Sharon could see who she was with. She was surprised at first, but being warmhearted, she said, 'Hello, Dr Goodison. Nice to see you.'

Lorna stood up, and for once she was lost for words. Sharon saw the stress in her face. 'Nay, you've been kind to me. It weren't your fault that I got arthritis, now, was it?' She put two and two together, and realised why the two doctors were there at the Council Chamber. She said with hesitation, 'If you don't mind, like, I'd like to wish you well.' And she held out her bent and twisted hand. There was complete forgiveness and humanity in the Lancashire girl's face.

'You're a good soul, Sharon.' Lorna's voice cracked. 'I'd like to know when the baby arrives, if you don't mind. I may not be here.'

Another voice broke in then. 'Dr Goodison.' A businesslike, impersonal voice. It was Dr Fielding, standing at the top of the steps. He descended slowly, giving nothing away, then, on the bottom step, his face broke into a smile, and he held out his hands.

Lorna could hardly speak as she shook it warmly. 'Oh, Dr Fielding.' As she stood with the old man, three other men came down the steps, and also shook her hand. Tessa stood back. She was no longer needed. She turned, and was just walking away along the High

Street, when she saw Adam's BMW draw up beside the chattering group. Lorna heard him, and as he stood up and came towards her she flew into his arms, calling his name. And as Tessa fled round the corner, the last thing she heard through the bustling traffic of Blackwood was the echo of Adam's name, hanging on the air in the strengthening sunlight.

She got in the car and pointed it towards Silver Birch Cottage. But she knew today was not the day for finishing curtains. Her mood was turbulent and lost. She felt like a lost soul, striving in vain for Paradise, and constantly being disappointed. She sat in the car for a while, trying to whip up enthusiasm for the half-finished archway that Billy was making for her. But the thought of roses round the door made her feel worse. 'The old maid's cottage,' she thought. There she would stay, growing older and more cantankerous, maybe. Maybe when she was old and grey, she would be made a Dame, for services to medicine. Then she could put it on her brass plate, on the gate under the roses . . .

It was after lunchtime, but she was not hungry. She sat musing, her thoughts a mixture of all that had happened to her since she came to Foxleigh. Running through them all was the figure of Adam Forrester. She knew nothing would be right until he had left with his bride for the States. And if she was invited to the wedding she must make hasty arrangements not to be there. It would be a grand affair, no doubt, the wedding of the year. Trust the Goodisons for that!

She was aroused by the roar of a Porsche engine that by now was familiar to her. Lorna was on the way back. In a hurried dash to escape from a painful encounter, Tessa started her car and made off in the opposite direction. She put her foot down and drove, swerving

round corners, and narrowly escaping executing a flock
of sheep.

She drew up with a screech of brakes at the farm at the
foot of Windmill Hill. The walk looked invitingly de-
serted. Yes, that was the place. Nothing but emptiness,
like herself, communing with trees and new bracken,
may blossom and ecstatic birdsong. She could lean
against the warm grey stone of the windmill and think of
nothing until opening time.

She was wearing a flowery cotton dress with a full skirt
and long sleeves. Her hair hung loose, and as she
brushed past the late catkins and the early damson
blossoms it became golden with pollen and decorated
with petals. But she was unconscious of her own beauty,
as she tramped between the dried furrows made by the
tractors, ignoring the strong smell of manure, as Farmer
Darlington drove past with an empty trailer.

'Arternoon, Doctor. Could do wi' a drop o' rain,
couldn't we?'

'Yes, we could indeed.' There it was, her professional
voice, cool and confident in spite of the hurt inside her
body. Come to think of it, she was a grower herself now.
Her newly bought runner beans and seed potatoes could
do with a drop of rain. 'Yes, indeed.'

The cow parsley on both sides of the path smelt
heavenly. With tall buttercups dotted amongst it, the
way upwards appeared to be adorned with gold and
silver lace. The scent of the hawthorn, too, was heavy
on the air, successfully blocking the aroma from Mr
Darlington's trailer. The sky between the trees was deep
blue now, with a few fluffy clouds that matched the clean
white fleece of the new lambs that wandered about on
the hillside, and bleated plaintively for their dams.

Tessa came out from the now foot-high new bracken,

with its lovely bright fresh green, right to the top of the
hill. There was no wind, and the air was kind and warm.
She tried not to think of the first time she had climbed up
here, when she had seen Lorna and Adam embracing.
Thank goodness they would soon no longer be part of
Foxleigh. Then it would be livable in again. She
breathed in deeply, looking far out over the Irish Sea.
Past the horizon was the Isle of Man, then Ireland, and
then, beyond that, was America . . . Tessa turned away
suddenly. It must be the distance that made her eyes
water . . .

There, that was better. She could see past the ruined
windmill the fields spread out like some lovely, un-
earthly patchwork quilt. Those light green patches were
fields of new wheat; the darker ones were winter wheat,
more mature. The brown fields were waiting for their
vegetables, their military rows of tiny cabbages and
cauliflowers and potatoes. And interspersed like some
phosphorescent jewels were the yellow fields of oilseed
rape, their vibrant colour almost hurting her eyes.

Tessa sat down on a patch of dry moss at the foot of the
windmill. The stones were warm and comforting to her
back. She closed her eyes, and listened to the shimmer-
ing song of the skylark, and the louder, more insistent
fluting of a thrush. She sighed. One day, when she was a
little old lady, she might find that this throbbing, bitter
pain might leave her alone. One day. The tears oozed
from her closed eyelids. Oh yes, it hurt. Dear God, it
hurt so much. Love was a funny thing, to be able to
wound so deeply, so very cruelly, and yet show no
scars.

'Tess! Tess, where have you been?'

She jerked her eyes open. Yes, it was Adam himself,
not some conjured vision from the depths of her despair.

She hastily shook the tears from her cheeks. 'What are you doing here?' she gasped.

He flopped down beside her and wiped the sweat from his forehead. His hair still needed cutting, but his presence was so bitter-sweet. He had come to twist the knife in the wound—unintentionally, of course. 'What do you think I'm doing? Looking for you, of course. I've got the afternoon off, and I wanted to see you, as soon as the hearing was over.' He looked round at her, and his eyes were dark blue and misty. 'I've driven all over this county, practically. I was sure you'd be at the cottage.'

'That's nice of you. But why?'

'You don't sound very welcoming. Tess love, you told me you'd got over that pilot of yours. I thought—I honestly thought—that you'd begun to like me. Well, to be honest, I thought it might be more than liking.'

She regarded him gravely, her gaze direct. There was no pretence between them now; he hadn't come up here to play word games. 'You hoped? You're teasing me, Adam. You knew all the time that I love you.'

He met her gaze then, and a wild hope flooded through her. What was he trying to say? He said humbly, 'I didn't know, love, but I kept on hoping.'

She suppressed the glory that was making her heart beat fast and her hands tremble. 'Adam, where's Lorna?' Her voice was steady. She had to know this first.

'How do I know? She told me all was well, and thanked me for all I'd done. And that's that—all over. I hope the experience has done her some good, that's all I can say.'

'She told you all was well, and thanked you,' repeated Tessa. 'What kind of a celebration is that? I thought you'd be taking her out to a champagne lunch, announcing your engagement to the world, that sort of thing. Not climbing hills to talk to strange women.'

'Strange women?' He looked at her and gently put his hand over hers in the soft grass. 'My darling, what engagement? Lorna Goodison is the last person in the world I'd want to marry!'

'But—'

He stood up suddenly, and looked out across the misty blue sea. 'I thought I loved her, once. We were unofficially engaged when I was an SHO. I thought I'd made it, dating a classy girl with a rich father. Then she gave me my first lesson in the school of hard knocks. I found her in bed with someone I thought to be my best friend.' He paused for a moment, while the skylark sang as though suspended in space for ever. He went on, his voice so low that she could hardly hear it, 'I never spoke to her again. Until this thing started—just before you came, in February. She came to me desperate, in tears, saying that her career was ruined—asked me for nothing but moral support, because she had no one else. Like a fool, I agreed.'

Tessa looked up at him, her eyes soft with admiration. 'That was a very decent, noble thing to do, after what she did to you. Oh, Adam, I thought—'

'What did you think?'

'I could see that you weren't exactly head over heels in love with her. But I thought—you were with her for her—money.' Her own voice was a whisper then. 'Forgive me.'

Adam turned away from the view and looked down at her. 'That's what you thought? Well, you and half the village, I expect. Nothing's secret in Foxleigh.'

'And she was flashing a big diamond ring.'

'Well, yes. If you'd asked me, I'd have told you. Her fiancé has been in Saudi Arabia, making lots of money so that they can buy a cosy little country practice in Surrey together. He's due back in June.'

A huge bumblebee buzzed clumsily round the windmill between them. Tessa leaned back against the comforting stones, feeling strangely shaky. So that was why Lorna was resigning! That was what Dr Fielding had meant by a certain young man who would take her away . . . Adam was not one scrap in love with Lorna. He didn't even want to see her again. And he had come here, searching her out until he found her. She looked up into his face, trying to read it. They had always been comfortable together, always sensed what the other was thinking. She wondered if he sensed her nervousness now.

'Well, Tess?' he queried softly.

'I'm not sure what I've got in the larder. But I was thinking of inviting you to dinner.'

His face relaxed into his lovely, easy smile, and her heart lifted to see the worried look gone for ever from his face. 'I don't need food. I can live on love.'

She scrambled to her feet. 'But you'll be going to America soon. What do I live on when you're in Washington?'

He shook his head. 'That's off. I refused the job as soon as I heard you were applying for the Senior Registrar's post at Foxleigh. Didn't I tell you? I figured that one of these days you were going to get over—you know, that Guy of yours. And when you did, I wanted to be around.'

'I wish you'd told me,' she sighed.

'I should have, but I didn't want to frighten you off by being too serious when you weren't ready.' Adam

walked across to the mill and sat down, lifting his face to
the sun. Tessa watched him, thinking that he was the
most wonderful person she had ever known. 'I might
have. I saw the angry look on your face the first time I
spoke to you—as though I was interrupting something
private, something secret.'

She nodded, looking down at him. He was twisting a
piece of grass now, not looking at her. She said, 'I
suppose I did think the world had died with Guy. We did
have a happy time together.' Adam twisted the grass,
kept his dark head down. Suddenly Tessa ran to him,
and he looked up. Yes, his eyes were gentle, and almost
as afraid as she was. She put her arms gently round his
neck. 'But, darling, you were there, day by day, all the
time, showing me—'

'Showing what?'

'Showing what a real man was like. Showing me that
happiness for me was Adam-sized, Adam-shaped, and
Adam-coloured. I realised in time that Guy and I would
have parted, as soon as we spent more time together. He
didn't like the things I liked. And he was always jealous
of my work.'

He put his arms around her waist, and she felt them
trembling. Suddenly they held each other very tightly,
comforting each other, and soothing away the pains of
the past. Tessa stroked Adam's hair as he pressed his
face close, kissing her breasts through the fine lawn of
her dress. He murmured, 'How long have you known?'

'Known?'

'That I would—do?'

She smiled down at the top of his head. 'Why do you
think I took off to a place of my own? Only that I
couldn't stand being so close to you, knowing that you
were going to marry Lorna. I'd lie awake at night,

listening for your step on the stairs. I'd wait for your key in the lock, wonder when you sighed if it was from happiness.'

'That's why you moved away?'

'Yes. I knew there'd be no peace of mind for me while you were there.'

He caught her into a hard embrace then, kissing her lips with a passion she had only thought about, preventing any more words. She lay for a second, luxuriating in the strength and power of the love that enfolded her so sincerely, then she began to kiss him back, giving him the reassurance that he wanted, that her passion and her devotion were as deep and unending as his.

He said in a husky voice, 'So, you lay awake and listened for me coming home, did you?'

'Yes. Just like being married, isn't it? Wondering where your husband is, wondering who he's been with?' He stopped her mouth with more kisses.

'So that's what you think of marriage, is it? Suspicion and worry?'

'I don't know.'

'Will you give me a chance to show you what it can really be like?'

'I will, if you will.'

He lifted his head and spoke with his lips against her cheek. 'There's nothing in the world I want more.'

'There's room in my cottage for two,' Tessa told him, 'But they would have to be very friendly.'

Adam looked up at her then, and they laughed together, full of wonder and trust. He whispered, 'We're friendly.'

He stood up and held out his hand for her, pulling her into an embrace, before suddenly lifting her bodily, and beginning to run towards the path. Laughing, she clung to his neck and said jerkily, 'But wait, darling. There's no room for two cars.'

Breathlessly Adam retorted, 'There's no nursery either, I'll bet. But we can take care of those details when we come back from our honeymoon. How about Washington?'

He put her down gently, as they neared the farm-house, and hand in hand, they walked down the path, oblivious of the rutted furrows, the smiling farmer at his door, the fresh beauty of the beech trees, that dappled their path with sunlight.

4 Doctor Nurse Romances
FREE

Coping with the daily tragedies and ordeals of a busy hospital, and sharing the satisfaction of a difficult job well done, people find themselves unexpectedly drawn together. Mills & Boon Doctor Nurse Romances capture perfectly the excitement, the intrigue and the emotions of modern medicine, that so often lead to overwhelming and blissful love. By becoming a regular reader of Mills & Boon Doctor Nurse Romances you can enjoy SIX superb new titles every two months plus a whole range of special benefits: your very own personal membership card, a free newsletter packed with recipes, competitions, bargain book offers, plus big cash savings.

AND an Introductory FREE GIFT for YOU.
Turn over the page for details.